Falling
FOR
ROMEO

By

JENNIFER LAURENS

Grove Creek Publishing

A Grove Creek Publishing Book/published by arrangement with the author.

FALLING FOR ROMEO

Second Edition / 2009

Grove Creek Publishing, LLC, 1404 West State Street, Suite 202
Pleasant Grove, UT 84062

Cover artwork: Sapphire Designs
Book design: Julia Lloyd, Nature Walk Design

ISBN:1933963948
Printed in the United States of America

for Jennifer

Falling
FOR
ROMEO

ONE

She looked into his eyes, nearly tasted his breath he was so close. Jennifer's gaze dropped to John's lips, full and glistening. He was utterly focused on her, as if nobody else mattered, as if they were alone. As if this moment wasn't real, but a dream. But it was real. And real was being watched by a bunch of panting, hormonal teenagers and one very demanding director.

John's hands, poised at her waist, sent an unexpected tingle through Jennifer's body when his fingers shifted. His breath smelled of spearmint. She heard a cough somewhere out in the auditorium but didn't dare break character just to try and see through the spotlight. The rest of the cast was out there watching—a sea of black.

Part of her wanted what was about to happen. She couldn't deny the warm jittering in her blood that had little to do with playing Juliet. She'd never been able to hide how she really felt about John. Now they stood as Romeo and Juliet, ready to kiss. Her heart thumped wildly, her hands were cold and stiff.

John is going to kiss me.

John looked into her eyes with the pained, obsessive love that Romeo carried for Juliet. She was supposed to return the needy look with one of her own, and she had been—until she thought about the absurdity of it. Her and John? She broke out in a nervous laugh.

"All right, everybody take seven," Chip called from the control booth in the back of the auditorium.

The house lights went up. John dropped his hands from her waist and took a step back, scowling at her. It didn't stop her laughing. She didn't care that she'd irritated him. In fact, it pleased her. She loved digging under his skin. What she did care about was holding up the rehearsal and angering Chip.

She held up a hand. "Sorry." She took in a deep breath to gain her composure. John waited, arms crossed, head cocked. "Oh, get over it," she snapped.

"You're being unprofessional."

She taunted, "This from somebody who's making his big debut?"

John rolled his eyes.

The stage came alive with crew adjusting the sets and Jennifer took in a sigh of relief. Any time she could buy from the awkward intimacy she had to create on stage with John, she would take.

She waited for Chip to hop onto the stage. The director's normally round green eyes were slit underneath one tightly knit brow. She'd learned that when he twisted his mouth he wasn't happy.

Putting a hand on each of their shoulders, Chip brought the two of them in close for one of his director chats. Jennifer frowned as her eyes met John's, and he frowned right back.

"Sorry, Chip," she said again.

"You're ready to do this, guys."

Jennifer made herself nod, though it wasn't true. No

one had to know she was petrified. She was an actress. She would have to act like the very thought of kissing John Michaels was not going to expose the fact that she had never been kissed. And she would try to ignore the thrill building in her veins.

"Let's try it again, with the kiss this time," Chip said. Everyone both onstage and off took their places.

Jennifer stood as if sentenced to the guillotine. It was John who took the first steps back to his mark, challenge electrifying his blue-green eyes for Jennifer to do the same. Mirroring his look, she took her mark.

"Whenever you're ready guys," Chip called.

Jennifer had never kissed anybody before. And she hated that John would probably know that and make fun of her.

She swallowed. *Oh no, I can't.* Her mind flashed with memories of him—the boy who lived next door. They'd played house, spent hours pretending to be pirates, cowboys and Indians. Even joined blood in a childish ceremony meant to bind them forever. He was the boy she'd loved to hate because he was always first, always smarter. Always better. Her heart fought her own feelings for him.

She stepped closer, until she felt his chest against hers. *I can do this. I'll show him.* He put his hands on her waist and she smelled his skin, his sweat, the mint on his breath.

"Your line just before the kiss, John," Chip directed.

As Romeo, John's look was desperate, desirous. Everyone in the cavernous room waited. But instead of speaking, he lowered his head, looking at the floor.

He'd forgotten his line.

Of course it was on the tip of her tongue, but something inside of her enjoyed his discomfort and she kept her mouth zipped.

He looked at her with a flash of pleading, as if asking her to save him. Only the slightest crease in her lips gave away that she never would.

Then his face relaxed. *"Oh blessed, blessed night! I am afeared, being in night, all this is but a dream, too flattering sweet to be substantial."* His eyes danced because he'd remembered. His hands tightened at her waist and then he drew her against him and her body sparked inside. As his head dipped to hers, her last thought was to stop him.

The thought dissolved when he covered her mouth with his. A hot tingling went to her bones. His mouth was warm. She'd not known what it would be like—kissing— but she hadn't expected anything like this, soft and sweet. As his lips pressed hers, they moved, as if exploring, urging her to kiss him back. Instinctively she lifted her arms around his neck. Every part of her focused on the gentle suppleness of his mouth.

Her knees melted.

Then the loud speaker crackled. "Jenn? John?"

Air cooled her lips. Feeling like she'd just been torn from the coziest dream, she blinked hard. Still in John's embrace, she tipped her head back to look out into the blinding lights.

"That was great, guys," came Chip's voice. "We might have to shorten it up a little, though."

John's arms loosened and he took a step back. She couldn't stop looking at him. He'd kissed her. She'd kissed him. His eyes were sharp—a mix of daring and wonder.

And she wasn't sure if the expression was Romeo's or John's.

.   .   .

Jennifer drifted in a fog, unable to snap into the clarity needed to finish the rehearsal. She couldn't take her eyes off of John. She waited offstage and watched him run his scenes with Fletcher Rigby, who was playing Benvolio. Still feeling the kiss on her mouth, she stood with her fingers pressed against her lips.

And there was John – reciting his lines as if nothing had happened.

Of course, he'd been acting when he'd kissed her. It was nothing more than that.

When the scene ended, she was embarrassed that her eyes followed him. As always, he was immediately surrounded by other cast and crew members, like groupies at the feet of a rock star. It didn't matter if the spotlight was on him—he was on stage even when he wasn't on stage.

Fletcher Rigby bounded over and took her in his arms. The strong musky scent of body odor filled her head. Dropping her into a dramatic backbend, he leaned close, smiling. "Hello my love, you did mahvelously."

Jennifer batted her lashes. "Why thank you, kind sir." She played along as they all waited for Chip to come backstage for what he called his 'roundup'.

Fletcher pulled her up and twirled her out in a spin. Part of the cast and crew now circled them. They wanted to know what that kiss was like, but only a few would be bold enough to actually ask.

"Oh, my gosh." Taunia Lakendale—the wardrobe mistress—too plump to have won a role onstage, she hung out backstage taking notes as the production neared performance time. "What was it like? It was so freaking *long!*"

The girls in the cast surrounded Jennifer with eager ears and anxious smiles. This was her chance to let loose a hive of vengeful bees. She'd never been much of a beekeeper. "Marginal, actually."

The admittance stunned the girls.

"Nuh-huh."

"No way."

"Seriously?"

Jennifer nodded, reaching into her purse. She pulled out her makeup bag for powder. It was a lie, but no one needed to know that. What was important was that she maintain her pride, that her next-door-neighbor turned man-of-the-hour think she was completely unfazed by the kiss. There was still that part of her that wanted to correct everyone's rosy-eyed vision of John. No one knew better than her that he was far from perfect.

"But he has such succulent lips," Lacey Naeverson looked over at him.

"Maybe he doesn't know how to use them," piped Trish Bigler. The girls didn't laugh or woo. Most were too shocked by the news and stared at John. He stood in the center circle of the boys, and casually glanced over.

"He's listening," Taunia warned.

Jennifer hadn't expected him to look over, let alone listen. He'd stopped paying attention to her since his name soared to celebrity status three years ago. That was when their past as neighbors and friends had changed forever. It still stung when she thought about it. She'd spent plenty of time trying to understand why childhood friends change course when they all seemed to travel the same road.

Though John was surrounded he kept that piercing gaze of his on her. She felt another rush, almost as hot as the one she'd felt when he'd kissed her.

"What was wrong with it?" Taunia asked. "I mean, did he use tongue or bite or something?"

"Yeah, was his breath rank?"

The pleasant memory of his mouth on hers, the sweet taste of spearmint, coupled with the fact that she hated that she liked the kiss, had Jennifer looking with distaste at her reflection in the compact. "The kiss was flat." She snapped the compact shut. "No juice in it at all."

"Course you know how this will sound," Trish inferred.

"Like truth."

"Like you're jealous."

Jennifer reached into her makeup bag for blush, even though her cheeks heated. She couldn't look the girls in the eye. She'd been called one of the best actresses that Pleasant View High School had ever seen, but she'd always had a hard time being a convincing liar. "Only because everybody thinks he's perfect."

"He is."

Jennifer rolled her eyes. "He's not."

"You'd tell? About the kiss?"

"If I'm asked."

The girls looked at her with a mix of admiration

and disbelief. None of them dared dispute her claim. It was her mouth John had kissed and that gave her momentary power. But in her stomach churned the discomfort of a lie that might spin out of control.

Focus quickly shifted from fascination of the kiss to Chip's entrance. He waved his notes overhead, half jogging in. "Okay, let's meet."

Quickly, the cast crowded around the tiny wooden desk Chip perched himself on. Jennifer made her way to the front and the cast parted until she rubbed shoulders with John. She looked up at him.

Something flashed in his eyes. Was it disappointment?

From the onset of production Jennifer had told herself she would be mature about everything—their lost past as well as their estranged present. Knowing they would have to work closely, she'd worked hard at treating him just like any other guy friend.

"Things went ten minutes over," Chip said.

"That kiss was ten minutes," somebody muttered and the group laughed. Jennifer tried to laugh along, saw that John's lips curved into a smile but no laughter left him.

Chip raised his hands to quiet everyone. "All right, all right. It's hard enough to remember all of the lines. Let's not put added pressure on our principals. We're here to support them."

"Hey, Jenn. I'll support you." Drake Alread leaned toward her with his lips pursed before the boys playfully shoved him back.

"Guys, guys." Chip stood on the desk as if being taller would give him more command. "I need a megaphone," he mumbled. "Reread the entire play tonight. I know most of you can recite it in your sleep, but reading it from beginning to end will give everybody a sense of timing that will be instinctual in performance. Deal?"

Everyone groaned out, "Yes." Chip then pointed out a couple of other details before excusing the cast for the night.

"So." Lacey Naeverson, cast as John's mother, Lady Montague, hung close to Jennifer as she gathered her backpack. "Count yourself lucky, Jenn. I know a hundred girls who would give it up to be in your place." Deliberately she flipped back a chunk of her dark hair exposing bare, gleaming shoulders in her turquoise tube top. The very idea that so many girls were willing to give themselves to John bugged Jennifer. She looked at him. He was still surrounded, though the crowd had thinned some and gone home. As he slipped on his royal blue student council jacket she felt the familiar surge of resentment. He got whatever he wanted, whatever was out there, whether he wanted it, or not.

It was enviable, amazing and disgusting.

"If that was a preview of what to expect from John Michaels," Jennifer began loud enough so he could hear, "it wouldn't be worth it." Hoisting her backpack over her shoulder, she headed for the door. When the room fell to a hush, she didn't look back.

TWO

Jennifer pulled up in her driveway five minutes later, still tingling with the sweetness of revenge. Whether or not John or any of his pals had heard the comment didn't matter, though she felt pretty sure they had. She'd told Lacey, and that was tantamount to announcing it over the school's PA system.

Her mom had left the front room light burning, knowing how much Jennifer hated darkness.

Jennifer slipped the key into the lock just as she heard a car coming up the street. John. The old grey truck he drove made a steady choking sound as if on its last mile of life. He drove faster than usual, and that made her nervous. She wouldn't put it past him to storm over and chew her out.

When his headlights caught her in a piercing gleam as he parked, she looked over with a look meant to tell him she was not going to be intimidated. Rather than dart to safety inside, she paused in the door frame and watched him.

He got out of his car and slammed the door, his fiery gaze pinning her. But he didn't cross his yard. He strode quickly to his front door, eyes never leaving hers, before he disappeared inside.

She heard the thud of the door shutting and sighed.

Guilt festered, mixing with a strange longing inside

of her. Years ago, she and John had spent hours talking out their bedroom windows—two windows which happened to parallel each other on the second floors of their homes. They'd strung string and spoken through empty cans and traded messages on a pulley system John had devised.

They were best friends.

Before turning on her bedroom light, Jennifer stood in the darkness and a shiver of discomfort ran down her spine. She peered at his window. It was black.

Having a panoramic view of each other's rooms had only been embarrassing once. After that, she always made sure her shades were closed *before* she undressed.

Her eyes adjusted to the darkness and she wondered where he was. The other windows of the house were dark; she guessed the rest of the family was probably asleep, like hers. Where was John?

She stepped closer to the window and the moonlight barely caught her in its silvery blue light, reminding her of a night she'd been afraid for him. He'd been sick with the mumps. As his face swelled, her young heart had thought her best friend might choke and die. He'd assured her he'd just swallowed baseballs.

Jennifer smiled. His light sense of humor was part of what drew people to him. He made you feel okay even if things weren't. That night he'd run a string from her window to his and told her to sleep with the window open, to tug on the string which he'd wrapped around his wrist. He'd do the same if he thought he was going to die.

Jennifer didn't dredged up these memories for a reason—they hurt.

Staring blankly into the darkness of his bedroom, she thought she saw movement. Striving to see more clearly, she stood even closer to the window, forgetting that she was in full view with the moonlight overhead. Her eyes blinked hard at what she thought she saw. She had to be absolutely sure.

John stood just inside the darkened window. Then he moved himself so the blue-ice glaze of moonlight hollowed out his cheeks and hardened his gaze to cold marble. No glee lingered in her blood from earlier that night now.

She needed to apologize.

But apologies were another thing that had come between them.

Pride made her reach out to close her shutters on his face, but even as the idea flickered in her mind he pulled his closed first

• • •

"You're late."

John turned, and found his father standing in his doorway. A flash of panic squeezed in his chest. He glanced at his watch. Eleven-thirty. "Practice went over."

Displeasure was evident in the hard lines on his dad's face. He still wore his work clothes: white shirt and dress pants. The tie wasn't even loose, so John knew his father hadn't taken the time to do anything but eat and go right back to work in his office when he'd gotten home from his job.

"I thought Chip was going to be better about letting you kids out on time. He knows you all have other responsibilities. Your jobs aren't getting done around here and it's hard on your mother."

John worked a knot out of his throat with a hard swallow and nodded. "I know."

"What about school work?"

"I'm all caught up, if that's what you mean."

"Your grades better not suffer because of this play, John."

"They won't, they aren't."

"I wonder how much time you're giving to your future when you spend so much time in these extra-curricular activities." His father stood in heated silence.

John's armpits began to sweat. He hated when his dad did this; stared at him like he was deciding whether he should scream at him or slug him. It had been years since his dad had hit him, so he really wasn't worried about being struck. And even if his dad did choose to hit him, this moment wasn't all about the fact that he was late again. For a second he forgot his nerves and his own frustrations bubbled.

He hated money problems—they infected everything.

His father's stare never wavered. "Is that all you have to say to me?"

What else could he say? He hadn't been late on purpose. He'd raced home and come right inside even though he wanted to go next door and demand some answers from Jennifer.

But John knew why his father waited. And saying the words his dad wanted him to say right then were a lot harder than any lines of dialogue he'd had to memorize. He couldn't look at him; didn't want to see the satisfaction in his dad's eyes. Words wouldn't change what was troubling his father inside. Only money could do that.

"I'm sorry." John let a few seconds go by before looking at his dad, sure the glimmer of victory would be gone, but it was still there and he bristled. Their fights were always like this, silent battles for control. He couldn't pinpoint when it had started, only that lately every time he and his father were in the same room they might as well have been entering a boxing ring. Their taut relationship was one of the reasons John spent every ounce of energy he had doing everything right—so he wouldn't get in trouble or upset his dad somehow and then have to apologize. Early on he'd figured out that if he made everybody happy things were smooth. That was the way he liked things. But even that was never enough for his dad.

"Don't let it happen again or I'll put you on restriction." His dad turned and left, closing the door behind him.

Anger and frustration pulsed through John's veins. *Yeah, you'd like that, wouldn't you? So I'd be stuck here and you can unload all your grief on me.*

He pulled off his shirt, balled it in two tight fists and threw it at the door.

The weapon was heavier than it looked. John held it carefully. For weeks they'd used wooden imitations for practice. After Chip's detailed instructions and warning about the use and cost of the rented rapiers, not to mention the insurance release forms they'd all had to sign, none of the guys dared take the first swing.

As the muscles in his arm carried the weight, John realized he could never show fatigue. *It'll get easier.* The more you did something, the natural result was that it became easier.

He counted on that.

Standing on stage with Connor, playing Tybalt, and Andrew, cast as Paris, he wondered if any of them thought the weapons would present a challenge. He was the first to lift his. Holding his left arm in position he pointed the sword at Connor. *"A right fair mark, fair coz, is soonest hit."*

Immediately Connor and the other boys took up their weapons, tapping each other's tips in a playful fight.

"This is nothing," Andrew stabbed at John's stomach.

Dancing back, John grinned. "Ten bucks says I'm the last one standing."

With wild hoots, the boys took the challenge. Each waved their weapons in John's direction. He darted out of the way, barely conscious of the crew and cast slowly gathering in the auditorium to watch. Sweat pearled on his brow. Minutes clicked by. One by one, the boys sloughed off in exhausted, embarrassed heaps to the side of the stage. Only Andrew remained. John's grin faded to a jaw set with determination. He locked eyes on Andrew. He jabbed and lunged without any sign of slowing.

His right arm ached, but he thrust anyway. A shot of adrenalin kicked in. He focused on Andrew's tiring form, on winning. In a last burst of energy John growled, giving the next few spears all he had and knocking the sword from Andrew's hand, leaving Andrew cursing.

The auditorium cheered, applauded and John heard the chant of his name—John, John, John— an odd ritual that accompanied anything public he did lately. Facing the seats he took a good-natured bow.

Quickly, he strode over and extended his hand to Andrew. Andrew worked to his feet and the boys slugged fists.

John scanned the audience. Jennifer was looking at him, he felt her gaze even from the stage. She stood inside the auditorium doors. Had she caught the fight? She sat in the audience with some of the girls. He hoped they weren't talking about him. It still burned to think of what she said about the kiss. The worst part was he couldn't understand why she said it. Did she think it was cake kissing her? He sweat just thinking about it. Pressing the tip of the sword to the stage floor, he spun the weapon to distract himself. He'd only kissed two other girls, but neither had been as scary as kissing Jennifer. She was…Jennifer.

He glanced at her again. She chatted animatedly with Lacey and Trish. Her blonde hair was pulled up in a floppy pony tail at the top of her head. He remembered her wearing it that way when they were kids. He'd pulled on the silken lock more than once to keep her in her place.

He grinned.

But the grin faded. Even if they hadn't hung out for a while, what she'd said was rude. He'd never say anything like that.

Last night he debated going over and chewing her out. If it was any other girl he would have. He expected her to know better. She'd been his best friend. Once.

Chip had the boys run through the fight scenes with the real rapiers again. John was grateful for the distraction. The play was a dream for John and his friends; boys balancing on the razor's edge between being boys and being men. To fight with swords, dance with girls and romance Juliet, well, it was all pretty cool.

His friends thought he tried out for the play because they all dared each other. In the deepest corner of John's mind the real reason was completely his own.

Jennifer.

What would an extra two hours a night cost him if it meant he could hang nearer to her? When Chip cast him as Romeo, he was stoked, hoping for an opportunity to be her friend again.

He was so involved in school the last few years he didn't analyze their drift. Then one day he saw her doing the most ordinary thing—opening her locker—and he glanced over. His heart beat hard in his chest at the sight of her smile. At the way her blonde hair shimmered.

After that, he tried to figure out what was going on with her, catching what he could from covert sources: her little brother and sister, his mom, her mom. Occasionally her name came up in casual conversation with his friends, but Jennifer Vienvu carried a status at PVHS that was renowned. Exclusive. John smiled. She was only Jenn Vienn. He'd nicknamed her that years ago. Somehow she turned into this beautiful goddess no guy felt worthy to talk to, let alone reach out and touch.

John finished his fight scene with Andrew, aka Paris, and glanced out over the seats to see where she was. She was alone now. He took his sword and hopped off stage.

"Next time I'll nail you, Michaels," Andrew called from the stage. He angled his rapier at John who gave him a mock salute before continuing down the aisle.

John went to the row of seats in front of Jennifer and sat. She'd been Jenn Vienn once and he didn't see anything wrong with reminding her of that. After what she said about him, he figured it was time.

Jennifer's stomach jumbled watching the fight scenes. It was cool seeing the boys practice with the wooden rapiers, but the slick sheen, the sharp clanging of real rapiers swinging added an unexpected zeal to rehearsal.

The sight of John deep in concentration was awesome. His face pulled tight, leaving his jaw hard, his lips set. She was captivated by the liquid way his body moved.

He looked hot.

He glanced out into the audience once or twice and that flash of fire in his eyes stoked her heart. Every time he looked at her she thought of the kiss. Once, he looked over and she was sure that his gaze lingered, that there was a message there. Don't lose it, she told herself. *He can have any girl he wants and he most definitely has no interest in you.*

"Is it true?"

Startled, Jennifer turned around and stared into the faces of four girls she recognized as other students at Pleasant View High. They weren't in the play; no doubt a handful of John's fans who had wandered in for a peek.

"Is what true?" Rather than look at the girls, Jennifer watched the boys spar.

The girls were silent for a few minutes, like they lost their nerve. Then the one Jennifer recognized as the most public of the four sat forward, her elbows on the back of the seat next to Jennifer. Her eyes were glued to John. "That you kiss John in the play?"

"It's Romeo and Juliet, of course we kiss."

The girls exchanged glances, two whispered to each other. They leaned over the backs of the seats for more. "I hear he frenched you."

How twisted facts got on the barbed wire of a rumor. "What else did you hear?" Jennifer asked.

"That you slapped him."

"Yeah, and then you guys had a fight right in front of everybody."

"Is it true you guys dated once?"

"That's not what I heard, I heard they used to be friends—"

"But then John liked somebody else—"

"And then they never spoke to each other again."

A smile bloomed on Jennifer's face. She kept her eyes on John. The rumors were rumors she'd heard before. Truth was she and John had never dated. The closest they'd gotten to saying something special to each other was the silly ritual they recited when they were kids and joined bloodied palms.

She still carried the scar and Jennifer looked down at her hand and wondered if she turned John's palm over, if the white line identical to hers would be there.

"So, did he french you?"

All Jennifer knew about kissing she'd read in magazines and heard traded in whispers. But to have tasted it and felt it smooth and melting on her lips, John's kiss had surpassed anything she'd conjured up in her mind.

"John wouldn't french in front of an audience." She hadn't defended him since she could remember. Suddenly warm all over, Jennifer hunkered down in the seat and kept an unfazed façade on John and the boys on stage.

The girls, seeing that she was done talking sat back for a few moments, whispering. Jennifer strained to hear what was being said in spite of how she fought ignoring them.

When they finally got up and left, she took a breath. The kiss was out there, and more juicy rumors would circulate. Every girl liked to be the center of excitement. Jennifer was no exception. Playing Juliet to John's Romeo was the electric current lighting up the dull halls of PVHS now, bringing awareness of who she was to the galactic level of John Michaels, something she hadn't counted on when she'd auditioned for the play. But then she hadn't counted on him auditioning either.

As John sparred with the other actors, students and teachers meandered in and watched. John's presence always drew a crowd. Jennifer noticed that the girls moved closer to the front of the stage, to the fringe of stage lights where they probably hoped John would see them.

He's just a boy. But he wasn't like any other and that was why he was the center of everything. She thought back to when they were young. Even then he led rather than followed—like Peter Pan—and that confident air promised adventure as well as safety.

She'd never known anyone like him.

The canker of jealousy she always felt for him was still inside of her so she reached into her backpack and pulled out the book she was reading for honors English— *Pride and Prejudice*. She wouldn't play into the fascination the world held for John Michaels if she had the opportunity not to.

But her concentration waned. Her eyes drifted back to the stage just in time to see him hop down, sword still in hand, and stride her way. The air around him buzzed and sizzled as he approached. He sat in front of her. Every eye in the room was on them.

John never hunched. As if he refused to completely relax, he sat erect, ready to soak up whatever stimulus surrounded him. For the moment he sat facing forward, giving her the chance to really see the back of his head, and the strong curve of his neck. He always wore his dark hair short. For the play, he'd grown it out long, and the naps caused the hair to stand in feisty rebellion. It was shiny, like silken velvet. Her memory searched for the feel of it because she'd touched his hair years ago when they'd played. More than once she had brushed dirt from it. She even plucked a wasp out of it once.

As he sat in front of her he looked around, offering her an opportunity to catch his attention. She fought a smile and forced herself to continue reading the tedious book in her lap.

"Caught up on your chapters?"

His smooth voice comforted, like molasses and orange tea. Her insides spun. She casually looked up. His skin was without blemish, another thing she envied as she fought the occasional pimple. She'd needed braces and he hadn't—of course. Because he ran track, he always had sun-kissed skin, which now set his white teeth to brilliance. But it was his eyes that captivated her: colorful opals, mysteriously changing with the sun or storm or the color of his shirt. Sure, they were just John's eyes and she grew up looking into them but the affect was different now.

"Yes." She nodded and closed the book. Their past meant conversation was uncomfortable.

"You like it?" He kept his eyes on hers and the affect was somewhere between terrifying and thrilling.

"I like the story, but Mr. Darcy's starting to get on my nerves. He's so cocky and arrogant."

"Obviously you haven't finished it."

Of course he had, she thought and she opened the book as if ready to read again. "Skimmed a little, did we?"

He turned around fully and faced her, one arm casually draped along the back of the chair. He had gorgeous long fingers. Gentle looking hands. She blinked and tore her gaze away.

He shook his head. "I never skim—unless it's a textbook."

"And then you just read the bold or bulleted parts, right?"

His left shoulder lifted. For a moment, neither spoke. Jennifer wondered if he was going to say something more.

"You and Lacey friends?" he asked.

She shrugged. "Just with the play and all."

They both heard laughter but only she looked to see whose it was. The four-pack of girls had moved nearer to them, trying to get John's attention.

"Why?" she felt compelled to ask.

"That's what I want to know."

"What do you mean?"

"Why did you say that? About the kiss?"

John was mercilessly direct. Jennifer saw it with his friends, other students and even teachers. She saw his directness with everybody but his dad. She admired that he spoke up for himself.

She couldn't meet his gaze anymore so she looked at the book in her lap. He wanted an explanation, but all she felt was guilt for having said the kiss stunk. But she wouldn't admit it.

When he didn't say anything she wished somebody would come by and rescue her from the awkwardness. She finally looked at him when she realized a rescue wasn't going to happen. He studied her with a look that sent a luscious ribbon of heat to her middle.

"John, dude." Andrew was going over some of the choreography on the stage for the sword fight in which Paris is killed by Romeo. "Come here for a sec."

John didn't get up, rather held her in that heated gaze for another ten heart-pounding beats. Jennifer wondered if he wanted to say more.

Finally, he stood.

She couldn't help herself, she watched him join Andrew. Every eye in the auditorium now shifted to the stage. Blowing out a sigh, Jennifer gathered her things to go backstage.

She'd seen enough.

THREE

"Today's journal entry is up on the board. Get to it." Miss Tingey never paced when she instructed. She walked— calculatedly—in front of the class. If she sat, which was rare, she hiked one hip on the table piled with notebooks, papers and textbooks.

Miss Tingey looked like she still went to high school. She was one of those teachers who kids rearrange their schedules to have. Her classes were known for scintillating discussions and hard work. She graded tough but made sure everybody left her class in love with learning.

Jennifer looked at the words Miss Tingey had written on the board. *How do you feel about gossip?* Over the year, the class had covered a variety of topics for their journal entries followed by class discussions. The idea of the journal was to write a remembrance of where you were as a senior.

Jennifer adjusted in her seat so she could see John. He sat up front. Always up front, she thought cynically. He wrote voraciously in his journal and she wondered what he was writing about. Guilt kept the pen still in her hand.

Miss Tingey only allowed ten minutes to make their daily entries, so Jennifer looked at her paper—still blank except for a daisy she'd drawn at the top. She decided to take the daisy design down the full length so she at least looked as if she was doing something.

"Okay, let's talk about this," Miss Tingey started. "How do you feel about gossip?" She waited for hands to shoot up.

One did. Jennifer didn't need to see whose it was, the quiet hush falling over the room told her.

"Yes, John?" Miss Tingey herself seemed to light up when John spoke, Jennifer thought wryly.

"It sucks," John began, and the class laughed. But Jennifer didn't, feeling something build in her stomach. "Most of the time it's not true. And even if it is, why does the world need to know it? Whose business is it?"

Miss Tingey nodded. Other hands went up. She pointed to a girl in the back. "Yes, Jessica?"

"But people live off of it." Jessica tucked her dyed-black hair behind an ear punctured with half-a-dozen silver earrings. Her dark eyes were serious under heavy metallic eye shadow in electric blue. "It's like they don't have lives of their own so they feed off the lives of others."

The class shifted, murmured, some in agreement, others in distaste.

"I think people say stuff because they're bored," one girl said.

"Or jealous," another added.

"Or vindictive," John's tone was sharp. The room hushed. Jennifer looked over and found him staring right at her.

Miss Tingey sat on the edge of her desk with a smile and a nod at John's comment. "Yes. Why does revenge initiate gossip?"

"Because that person isn't there to defend themselves in the first place," John went on. "When you think about it, it's pretty wimpy."

Murmurs of agreement and amazement followed at a peer so intuitive. Jennifer felt the steady gaze of that peer still on her.

Miss Tingey looked for other comments and her gaze stopped on Jennifer. "Any comments? Jenn?" Usually, Jennifer and John verbally sparred during class discussions, trying to one-up each other. The class now turned expectantly to face her.

"I just think sometimes things are said that are misconstrued as gossip when what they really are is just an opinion."

"So what's the difference between gossip and opinion?" Miss Tingey stood, and began walking again.

Jessica with the studded ear sat forward and the chains on her black leather jacket banged against the metal desk. "Even though our opinions are our right, gossip's started with malicious intent."

"So let me see if I get this," Freddy, the himbo running-back shifted his bulky body in a desk that barely held him. "If I run thirty yards, but the ref only calls it at twenty-two and then everybody talks about it later, then that's gossip?"

It took the class a few minutes to stop laughing and when they finally did, John said, "If it hurts somebody, it's wrong. That's just it."

Almost everyone nodded in agreement. The guy sitting behind John lifted his hand to slap John's.

"Let's take it deeper." Miss Tingey stopped in front of the class, her chin thoughtfully held in her fingertips. "Is gossip gender specific?"

"What's that mean?" Freddy asked.

Dozens of voices filled the air at once, the whole

room a hive until Miss Tingey held out both palms and pressed them down as if pushing out the disruption.

Hands went up. John's went up. "It's more a girl thing," he said.

"Both sexes gossip," a girl piped, and immediately the boys disagreed.

"Not like girls."

"Guys don't talk about stuff like girls do."

"Girls don't have any boundaries."

"Yeah, they're mean, man."

"Yeah – cats." Freddy hissed, clawing at the air with his fingertips.

A girl up front raised her hand. When the class quieted, she glanced at John, fluttered her eyelashes and said, "Not all girls gossip. Real friends don't stab each other in the back."

Jennifer rolled her eyes and raised her hand. Miss Tingey nodded at her. "People gossip when it's convenient for them, no matter who they are."

"Convenient?" John's face twisted into sarcastic disbelief. He was looking at her again and the tight line between them pulled the class into a hard silence. "So that makes it okay?"

"You've never said something about somebody that isn't true?" Jennifer asked.

"Why would I? There's plenty to say that is true without having to make up something."

"Oh, so it's better to spread stuff around that's true? It's the same thing."

"How about you try keeping your mouth shut?"

Jennifer noticed the thick silence in the room. Every one was staring at them. Her cheeks heated and she turned away and faced Miss Tingey. Hearing palms slap in conquest made her angrier, but she didn't look over to see if John was a part of it.

He made her think. *Good.* The shocked way her eyes opened after he told her to keep her mouth shut was satisfying. Now John wondered what rehearsal would be like.

The auditorium was almost empty with the exception of a few random students who'd snuck in. When they saw him, they watched. John moved to the back of the room into darkness. It wasn't easy being watched all the time. Sometimes the pressure crushed, like being caught in a giant garbage compactor.

He took a seat in the furthermost chair.

Paint on the sets was fresh, filling the cavernous room with the pungent scent of turpentine underneath the hot lights. Cast and crew worked late into the night over the past few days building and painting the walls of the city, the lattice that Romeo climbed to reach Juliet, and the tomb where the two lovers took their final breaths.

They would kiss again today. He'd kiss Jennifer every day from now until the play ended.

His body hummed.

But the sting of her words flatlined the pleasant buzz. Did she really think the kiss was lame? The kiss had been far from lame—from his angle anyhow. It was better than when Tricia Boswell had shocked him with a kiss. And way better than when he'd kissed Sara Lahoney. Sara had been his first. They'd barely known each other and it had been a strangely empty experience.

Even in front of everybody, kissing Jennifer was unlike anything else. John figured it was because they'd known each other for so long. He thought that would make their stage intimacy weird, but lately he couldn't stop thinking about her.

Other cast members gathered in the darkened room and the usual scanning took place. Some saw him. Those who did looked eager to join him but hesitated. He didn't want company, so he kept himself in the dark and didn't meet any gazes. His stomach knotted. Four o'clock. He was within moments of facing Jennifer.

Any other girl didn't set his nerves on edge. It seemed every other girl went out of their way to agree with him. Sometimes he liked the convenience of that, most of the time he was bored by the predictability.

When Jennifer entered, John sat up. She didn't come in and look around like everybody else. Jennifer Vienvu didn't care if anybody watched her. John liked that. She did what she wanted. Even as a fresh victim of her opinion, or gossip—whatever it was, he liked that she had a voice of her own, not one that got lost in the screams of the crowd or whispered in unquestioning compliance with his.

She wore baby blue today. Her vanilla ice cream hair was down, melting around her shoulders. No expert on hairstyles, John realized that he liked Jenn's hair just about any way she chose to wear it.

Her light laugh caused a ripple somewhere inside of him and he shifted in his seat. She hadn't seen him yet. He may like her self confidence, but, hey, if she wondered where he was, she'd check around for him by now, wouldn't she?

Most of the cast had arrived and buzzed all over the room. It would be only moments before Chip flew in, and the energy level cranked to high.

John stood. A dozen heads turned his direction. He wondered if he could make it backstage without being approached by somebody wanting something. He weaved through the rows and noticed that Jennifer's head turned. Though he still didn't want to talk to anybody, not even her—yet, he forced himself to make eye contact with those watching as he walked down the center aisle of the auditorium.

"John." Ty, the set manager waved.

A hard slap to John's shoulder brought his face to Blake's. Still touching up the sets, the eager junior was splotched like a Dalmatian with paint. "Dude."

"Hey." John slugged his arm and continued his stroll toward the stage.

"Hi, John." The high pitch of female voices made John cringe. He turned to his left. A group of girls cast as the citizens of Verona huddled in some of the seats, grinning and giggling.

He gave them a smile. "Ladies." When they dipped their heads together in whispers he quickened his pace. Out the corner of his eye he caught Jennifer watching. A warm shot of pleasure went through his system. He jumped on stage with a little more finesse and stood under the fiery spotlight, ready for rehearsal.

John's cool professionalism created angst in Jennifer. She prided herself in being able to read people—guys, especially. She had no idea what he was thinking. Long ago, she'd figured out what she could get away with, how much she could say, how far she could go. It worked with just about every boy she knew—except one. For having known him so well, she realized she hardly knew him at all now.

With the exception of an occasional non-scripted glance, he all but ignored her. The kiss was coming, and the gradual gathering of butterflies in her stomach caused her palms to sweat. When he touched her, her clammy hands would give her away so she rubbed them against her clothing to keep them dry.

"Are you nervous?" Lacey whispered as the scene played out. Romeo and Benvolio were coming in secret to the party where Romeo first sees Juliet. Jennifer stood with Lacey and watched the dancers— Juliet yet unaware of Romeo's presence.

"Not at all." Jennifer didn't break character knowing that Chip watched from the director's booth.

"I dare you to bite him."

Jennifer's face twisted into shocked surprise at Lacey's wicked smile.

"Whatever." Jennifer concentrated on the scene so she wouldn't miss her cue. But a strange shiver ran along her spine. No way would she bite John, that was just weird. Just before she stepped into the action she heard Lacey whisper, "Do it."

Jennifer searched the partying, dancing crowd for John. He was easy to spot. That dark mop of unruly hair stuck out like a black bee in a hedge of flowers. He moved through the dancers with such purpose, the thrill racing through her pulse was not solely theatrical.

Juliet found her true love. He stood a few feet away amidst the music, the laughter and joy, a mere mask for two families with a rivalry that nurtured pride and refused love. But even with obstacles seeped in tradition, even with resistance, Romeo's determination drove him through the crowd to her.

When he stopped, his eyes locked on hers. Jennifer told herself she was Juliet, feeling what Juliet felt for Romeo. But that wasn't all. Though they'd been there in that very spot in other rehearsals, it was as if they stood there for the first time. Only she couldn't make her eyes see Romeo. John made her knees soft, her head light. When her lips broke into a smile, it was because her heart thudded one name.

John made his way through the dancers to Jennifer. Every nerve jittered. Within seconds he'd touch her. In a few more minutes he'd kiss her. His feet wanted to flee, but flowing in his blood was something he couldn't deny that he wanted.

He never ran from anything, least of all a girl. Still, everyone in the room was curious, titillated even by the physical romance unabashedly explored in Romeo and Juliet. That meant the spotlight that seemed to be his constant companion was heating up.

In this scene, he was supposed to go to her and take her hands. He was supposed to look into her eyes as if—*why was it so hard to think it?* For weeks, Chip had forbidden them to touch, insisting the wait preserved the chemistry needed to make the love story alive for performance. But to look into her eyes as if she was the only girl on earth, the one he wanted, needed—the nerves in his throat clutched. He wondered if he'd be able to deliver his lines.

"You okay?" Fletcher asked. He played Benvolio, Romeo's friend and sidekick. Together, they were crashing the Capulet party in search of Juliet.

"Fine." John swallowed. "Why?"

As staged, the two of them ducked behind four dancers. "Your face is white."

John took a deep breath and made his move across the front of the stage to Jennifer.

Juliet saw him and now waited. John's heart skipped. Sweet eagerness lit her face. Her blue eyes were happy, excited. The sight calmed him some and he thought that Romeo was a pretty lucky guy.

The stage was hot under the lights, the smell of sweat and fresh paint intoxicating. Music urged him forward; he hoped she wouldn't feel his heart beating in his hands. Reaching out, he took hers and noticed for the first time how delicate they were. Without thinking, he looked at them, and ran his thumb over her knuckles. Familiar hands. They'd climbed trees together, built mud cakes side-by- side.

He took her by surprise, touching her that way. A smile would have broken out on his lips had he not already had one—Romeo's. He stood under the heated lights, her hands in his, his voice ready.

And forgot his line.

Panic shoved euphoria right out of his system. Sweat

bled from his face. His mouth opened and nothing came. Thankfully, the dancers kept dancing, the citizens still played at being spectators. Unconsciously his grip on her hands tightened as his brain squeezed for the right words.

"What's my line?" he whispered.

The way her eyes danced, he knew he was screwed. She didn't tell him. Frustrated, he nearly shoved himself away. The music stopped, the dancers slowed and silence fell like a bad smell over the stage.

The heat of humiliation started in his neck and spread through his body. Turning from Jennifer, he hoped to hide what he knew would be a red face, but it was impossible to hide anything when you lived in the glare of a spotlight.

"I need the line, Chip," John barked into the darkness.

Chip's heavy sigh spoke volumes of annoyance. "We're days from show time, people," he began. John felt every eye from the cast burn into his back, and sharp rays from Chip hitting him in the chest, but he held his head up anyway.

"If you don't know your lines," Chip came down the center aisle, "then I don't want you doing anything else, and I mean anything other than eating, sleeping and peeing, until you do. Get it?"

Murmurs of agreement, nodding heads followed. Chip now stood at the front of the stage, looking up into John's face. "You," he said, "don't get to pee."

John didn't smile or laugh, even when Chip smiled at him first. He figured being unable to remember lines was inexcusable for an honor student, somebody on student council. A guy who had rented every version of Romeo and Juliet and watched each one to better understand what he'd gotten himself into. He memorized the whole script two weeks after he was cast—a feat for a guy who had a problem memorizing.

It didn't set well that his mind was now so easily distracted.

Out the corner of his eye, Jennifer shifted. He didn't look over. It was callous she hadn't prompted him. Now, he was mad.

"Let's take it from where you come in again, John," Chip announced. "Places." Then he stepped back into the darkness.

John looked over at Jennifer and scowled. Her baby blue eyes teased. *Yeah, I'm looking at you, babe. You could have helped me and you didn't.*

Storming back to his starting position, John tensed. *Why can't she ever forget a line? I'd love it if she was the one standing there with her mouth hanging open, looking stupid. I'd friggin' love it.*

Since she was Miss Perfect, he'd have to throw her balance off some other way. The ribbon of revenge dangled temptingly inside of him—a feeling he hadn't felt for her in a long time.

Music started. Its light, harmonious strains irritated John as stormy frustration built. Dancers bowed to each other. As he watched her in preparation for his move across the stage, he noticed that her back was to the audience. In her pretended excitement, her body moved as if she had an itch deep inside.

John waved his hands over his head. Everything stopped.

"John?" Chip asked.

"Yeah, I was just thinking." He took a feigned, thoughtful pose. "When Jenn's standing there with Lacey, isn't her back to the audience?"

Jennifer's eyes flashed; pink embarrassment flushed her face. He made her think. *Good.* He almost smiled.

"You're right," Chip said. "I missed that. Thanks. Jenn." Jennifer squinted out into the darkness. "Remember to cheat right there."

"And she's doing some wiggling thing," John added innocently, his hands gesturing to her bottom. When Jennifer shot around to him with a glare, it took everything he had not to break into a big grin. "Something with her, uh...her rear."

Everyone on stage erupted into laughter. John smiled. Chip walked toward the stage again, lips twisted in thought. "Let me see you in your last position, Jenn."

Obediently Jennifer stood ready. Only, with every eye pinning her, her body didn't move. "I don't think she knows she's doing it," John observed. "She gets so into it, it's like she's an excited puppy."

Jennifer's eyes opened wide. Red bled up her face. *That was too far.*

In an effort to calm the laughter and talk, Chip climbed up onto the stage and took Jennifer aside. John was instantly surrounded by the boys, all of who made jokes about his comment. But John couldn't take his gaze from Chip and Jennifer.

She looked—did she really look ready to cry? He felt like he was slugged in the stomach with a two-by-four labeled: *Loser.*

When Chip finished talking to her, she returned to her mark. Her chin was up, her eyes were cool and John saw no trace of the criticism anywhere. But Chip glanced at him with a biting look before jumping off stage.

FOUR

Jennifer hadn't cooled down. When she walked through the front door of home two hours later, she let everyone know it with a heavy slam. She stomped her feet across the living room toward the kitchen, though she had no intention of eating. She hoped her mother had ten or more dozen eggs in the refrigerator she could huck at John's window. If there weren't any eggs, her mother always kept a container of cottage cheese. With a large spoon, she could fire at will and make a nice, goopy mess that would harden and be impossible for John to scrape off.

Dinner was over hours ago, but the scent of roast, onions and garlic still hung in the warm air; comfort food that brought her no comfort tonight. The refrigerator was void of either item, and Jennifer slammed it shut with a perturbed sigh.

"How was rehearsal?" Her mother sat at the kitchen table organizing what looked to be hundreds of coupons. Her sandy blond hair barely hung to her jaw and was tucked behind her ears. Jennifer thought the sassy style made her mother look younger. She didn't dress old, either. Could have passed for a teenager herself, in fact, in her tight jeans and fitted sweater.

Jennifer looked over the scraps of newsprint. "Rehearsal was crappy." She never understood why her mother went through the ritual of clipping coupons; she'd never seen her use one.

"What made it crappy?" Deftly, her mother stacked the cereal coupons in prearranged piles and reached for the forty-five ounce soda she religiously kept at her side.

"I don't know." Jennifer slumped into a chair.

Maggie Vienvu sipped, studying her daughter. "You know all your lines, right?"

Jennifer nodded. Cautiously she placed her elbows on the table so they didn't disturb any of the well-placed stacks.

Her mother set down her drink. "Problems with Chip?"

"No, of course not." Jennifer noticed a stack of pet items and picked up a coupon for kitty litter. "We don't have a cat."

Her mother shrugged. "You never know. I was always bringing home stray dogs, cats. Fish."

Jennifer laughed and it felt good. "Fish?"

"From carnivals." Her mother began to place her perfect piles inside the red Velcro coupon holder. "John?" When her mother looked at her, Jennifer averted her eyes. "Just a guess."

"I want to kill him."

"I haven't heard that for a long time."

"Yeah, well, that's because he's been out of my life for a long time."

"Jenn, he never was out. He lives next door."

"Whose side are you on?" Jennifer reached over and grabbed her mother's cup, pausing for approval before taking a drink. Her mother nodded.

"There are no sides. There's you and him."

"You make it sound like something it's not."

"You mean like a couple?" Their eyes met. For a moment, Jennifer didn't like the way her mom's eyebrows lifted in a pleasant smirk. "You're Romeo and Juliet," she teased. Then she took the drink from Jennifer, sipped and handed it back.

Jennifer took a slurp before plopping the drink to the table. "He insulted me at rehearsal today. You wouldn't believe what he said."

"What did he say?"

"That I looked like an excited puppy."

A faint smile creased Maggie's lips. "How cute."

"Mom!" Jennifer's insides burst. "That is so—so—"
So typical. Her mother thought John could do no wrong. Ever since they were children and he came over with his, 'Yes ma'am, no ma'am, please, and, oh, thank you.'

"You're just like everybody else when it comes to him. You think he's perfect."

Maggie quickly filed the coupons nearest Jennifer. "He's not perfect. But he is one of the nicest, most polite, conscientious boys I know. Trustworthy, honest, help—"

"And the rudest." Jennifer crossed her arms, frowned.

"He was trying to be complimentary."

"He was being critical and rude. You don't know the context of the comment."

"It was probably just his way of showing that he likes you."

Jennifer's face heated. She turned, resting her chin on her crossed arms so her mother couldn't see. "He does *not* feel that way about me."

"Oh, he's liked you forever."

Because she couldn't believe what her mother said, Jennifer lifted her head and looked at her. There was nothing telling in the way she gingerly filed away the last pile of coupons, except the smile on her face.

Standing, Jennifer took in a breath that warbled out with embarrassing contentment. She hoped her mother didn't hear it. "I'm going to bed." She turned, hearing her mother take another sip.

"Pleasant dreams," her mother's sing-song tone teased.

Jennifer let out a sarcastic growl and continued up stairs.

The light was on in John's window, so Jennifer remained in the dark. From what she saw, he wasn't in his room. But she heard his voice. Quietly, she unlocked her window, slowly cranking the shaft so it swung open.

"But soft! What light through yonder window breaks? It is the east, and Juliet is the sun. Arise, fair sun, and kill the envious moon, who is already sick and pale with grief. That thou, her amid, art far more fair than she. Be not...be not...here...be...not her...."

Peering out over the ledge, Jennifer saw John down on the grass, looking up into his window. She squelched a giggle and stood back in the darkness so he wouldn't see her.

His soothing voice salved the cold night air. When his voice first changed, she'd teased him about it. Then one day she noticed how calming, almost melodic the cadence was.

She leaned against the wall, her hand over her heart, listening to him. Her lips curved into a smile.

"Be not her…"

Jennifer heard the line he stumbled on in her head and thought about whispering it out the window, but then she'd probably make him madder at her. He wasn't one to hold a grudge, but they weren't kids anymore. The social stakes were higher. He was unnecessarily mean at rehearsal, pointing out her cheat to Chip. She almost closed her window, leaving him to his exasperating rehearsal alone.

He deserves it.

"Be not her…crud."

But how could every bitter and angry thought that had festered inside dissolve at just the sound of his voice? She leaned out the window and looked down through the darkness at him.

Night brought a slight breeze into the valley. The shrubs and rose bushes sleeping alongside the Vienvu house rustled, as if refusing to wake from a winter dream. John's breath was soft, white, curling upward into the night.

"You have my lines down at least," she said.

Startled, John turned and looked up at her. "Yours and everybody else's but my own," he said on a sigh.

"Thought you could use some prompting."

"I could have used it this afternoon."

She should have frowned at the reminder of the unpleasant rehearsal, but he looked every bit the part of Romeo. She smiled. "Sorry about that."

The next moment warm wonder and promise seemed to be in the air, even with the biting temperature.

A tree in the Vienvu back yard twined its leaves with a tree in the Michaels' yard and the soft rustling was the only sound.

John took a step closer to the wall of her house. His gaze was intense. For a moment, Jennifer was afraid he was going to confront her about what she said about the kiss. She readied for a fight.

"*It is my lady,*" he began, his voice smooth and rich as melting honey butter. "*Oh, it is my love. Oh, that she knew she were! She speaks, yet she says nothing. What of that?*"

"*Ay, me!*" Jennifer replied, keeping from breaking into a giggle. Her insides spun.

John took hold of the lattice her parents had attached to the house some thirteen years ago. Now, it was covered with some sort of ivy. During the summer the growth was dotted with fragrant red blooms. With the chill of winter, the small green leaves browned and crisped, petrified by frost.

"*See how she leans her cheek upon her hand. Oh, that I were a glove upon that hand. That I might touch that cheek!*"

John's face glowed with the blue haze of a winter moon. He felt for a spot of security in the lattice with his foot. His hands dove deep into the growth without hesitation. He looked driven, eyes focused, body determined. He pulled himself up.

"*O speak again, bright angel!*" he continued, slowly climbing. "*For thou art as glorious to this night, being o'er my head, as a winged messenger of heaven.*"

Jennifer reached out both arms to him, just like she did in the play. "*O Romeo, Romeo! Wherefore art thou*

Romeo? Deny thy father and refuse thy name. O if thou wilt not, be but sworn my love, and I'll no longer be a Capulet."

With each pull, John drew nearer. Jennifer's heart fluttered. "Be careful," she whispered on a laugh.

"Fear not, Juliet." He grinned. "Not only am I Romeo, but I have been known to morph into Spiderman."

Jennifer leaned out further, extending her hand to help. Then they both heard a snap, followed by a sharp crackle. John's eyes shot wide. He slid and tumbled down, falling flat on the hard ground below.

Jennifer gasped and ran from her bedroom. Her mother was turning off the lights in the kitchen when she flew past.

"Jenn?"

"Be right back!" She was out the back door and around to the side of the house before she took another breath. The breath she sought choked in her throat. She stopped, the sight of him freezing her.

"John?" Her heart pounded. He lay like the dead, eyes closed, body still. His face, just moments ago a glow with the moon's milky reflection, now looked pasty.

Dropping to her knees, she knelt over him, unsure of what to do. Her eyes blurred. She blinked fast, her throat burning. "I—John? Oh, no." Gently, she reached out and touched his shoulder. "John? Are you okay? John?" She nudged him with both hands. "Come on, wake up. You can't be hurt."

His head moved a little and she sucked in a breath. He grimaced, his dark lashes fluttered. Letting out a groan, he lifted his hands to his head for a moment before they trembled back to his sides.

Panicked, Jennifer grabbed the hand closest to her and squeezed it to her breast. "Are you hurt?" She leaned over his face. "John?"

"My head." He rolled toward her. "Something...my head...it's..."

"What? John, talk to me." She pressed her hand to his forehead and stroked the side of his cheek. "I better go get my mom."

Snapping his hand around her wrist, John shot up with a laugh.

Jennifer fell back on her butt, her pounding heart robbing her voice. Fury and relief whirled inside of her. She wanted to slap him and hug him. And yet the indescribable warmth of gladness caused tears to spring from her eyes.

"You should see your face." His laughter died. He went perfectly still.

Unable to stop the cache of tears escaping her, Jennifer scrambled to her feet, ready to escape back to her house when he shot up next to her.

"Hey." He set a hand on her shoulder. Comforting warmth shot down her arm, through her stomach and to her toes.

"That was so mean."

"I know. Sorry. Really, I am. Are you okay?"

"No, you retard. You scared me."

His hand left her shoulder and she felt a chill. John lifted his arms for examination, looking at the dirty, leaf-infested sleeves of his student council jacket. "Oh, man. Look at this. This thing costs fifteen bucks to dry clean."

Jennifer shoved at him lightly. Just touching him

made her feel better. "You could have broken your neck."

"Nah." He looked up at her window. "If that wood wasn't so old, I could climb up there anytime." His eyes lowered to hers.

Jennifer took a deep breath. "Yeah, well, it is old and you need to keep your neck in one piece, Romeo." The moon hid behind some stringy clouds and suddenly the night was very dark. Jennifer heard him breathe; smelled the faint scent that was uniquely his.

As children they spent hours out in the mysterious world of nighttime. Together they'd laced toilet paper over neighbor's bushes, engaged in games of hide and seek, of chase. But tonight he looked entirely different than the boy she'd played games with under the moon's watchful eye. Tonight he breathed erratically, not from the exertion of play, but from something that stirred her deep inside.

He took a step toward her. Afraid to move, she didn't. She didn't want anything to change. Nothing could stop what she hoped in her heart he was going to do. But it didn't matter if he kissed her or not. She could stand there forever, just looking at him.

His arms moved, as if reaching out for her. They heard the crunch of grass.

"Jenn?" Her mother.

Jennifer whirled around. Her mother stood with her hands tightly clutching herself against the chilly air. "Oh, I didn't see you, John."

"Hi, Maggie."

"You two okay?"

Jennifer nodded. A soft heat radiated into her

back. John. She hoped he wouldn't move, that after her mother left, she'd turn around and everything, the moment, the moonlight, would all be as it was seconds ago.

"It's eleven forty-five," Maggie said, then turned. "Just in case you thespians want to know." Grass crunched under her feet as her mother disappeared around the corner of the house. The sound of the front door shutting was distant.

Jennifer turned back around and knew the moment was lost. Looking up into John's face, she saw by his sober expression John knew it too.

"You sure you're okay?" She took a chance and touched his head, just above his left ear. The softness of his hair brushed her fingertips. Then she tucked her hands into her arms and folded them across her chest.

The way he held her with that penetrating gaze of his mystified her. Don't let it get to you, she thought. It doesn't mean anything. Neither spoke for a time until she finally took a step back. "See you tomorrow."

"'Night, Jenn."

The locust trees in the front yard shimmied, sending leaves scattering at her feet. She thought, as she walked around the corner of the house and took a deep, cold breath, that there might not ever be another moment like that one. But tomorrow was another day—another rehearsal.

Jennifer didn't consider herself a moody, depressed soul, yet she didn't make excuses for her moods—they made her a better actress. The euphoric jittering streaming through her was incredibly delicious. Her mind flashed scenes of John last night in the moonlight, climbing up her wall, reciting his lines. *If one night has left me like this, I'm really hopeless.*

She walked down the hall crushed between hundreds of other bodies as students headed toward the gymnasium for an assembly. Her smile electrified her face. She passed the glassed-in offices of the school's administrators and couldn't resist a peek at her reflection.

Pretty hot.

To her right, a group of freshman playfully hit each other and one of them rammed into her, sending her sideways. If it was any other day she might have sent them one of her disparaging, *grow up* looks. Today, she ignored the immature expression of friendship.

Nothing could penetrate her perfect day.

"Heard John frenched you at rehearsal the other day."

Jennifer recognized the deep, honeyed voice of her best friend, Rachel Baxter. Rachel shared Jennifer's love of theater, as well as their mutual fascination with the male species.

The nasty rumor nearly poked a hole in Jennifer's effervescent mood. Somebody stepped on her toe. "Hey, watch it!" she snapped. "No, he didn't. I can't believe the way rumors get twisted around here."

"I was so stoked for you."

Jennifer stopped. "Why should anything John does stoke me?"

"Come on, you've had it for John since I first met you."

"I have not." For a moment, the crowd stopped,

stuck in the door of the gym like a plug, and Jennifer choked on the smothering closeness. In reality, the choking sensation had more to do with what Rachel said than the bodies pressing into her.

Rachel looked at her with a raised brow. The body-jam wasn't budging. Somebody behind them had eaten onions for lunch. A boy to their left was chewing gum, it clacked and popped in Jennifer's ear. The worst was the kid in front of them whose neck blistered with juicy acne. Jennifer grimaced.

"So." Rachel leaned close. "Word is he stinks."

Guilt rushed Jennifer all over again. After last night, she had to send another piece out into the web of school gossip to correct what she'd sent out about the kiss. "I never said that – exactly."

They pushed through the doors. Zit-boy still remained in front of them and Rachel took Jennifer by the arm and led her away. "Then what was it like?"

For a second, Jennifer thought of confiding in her best friend. "It was…"

"Rachel! Jenn!" Spencer's tall, rangy form shot up from the crowds filing onto the bleachers. The basketball player was hard to miss. "Seats." He gestured to his sides where his friends, some of whom were considered the hottest at school, sat hunched over, elbows coolly set on their knees, requisite boredom on their faces.

Jennifer and Rachel made their way to the coveted spots, wiggling in between Cort Davies and Alex Jesperson, both who played first string for the Pleasant View Vikings football team.

"Hey guys." Jennifer flipped her blonde hair over her shoulder with a flirty smile. Rachel squeezed in between

Cort and Spencer. "This topic is not closed," she told her.

"What topic?" Spencer leaned nosily over Rachel's lap. Used to being pawned over, Rachel simply sat back to allow for better conversing for all of Spencer's friends now casually perked to attention, their athletic bodies flexing as they turned in their seats.

Jennifer shot Rachel a silencing look, but surrounded by adoring guys, Rachel missed it completely.

"I heard you got on John Michaels," Spencer said.

This rumor seems to have a life of its own, Jennifer thought with disgusted fascination. Five seconds ago, she'd been frenched by John.

Spencer tried being cool by not staring as he waited for her reply. Jennifer didn't know what to say, and was relieved when Principal Ackerman cleared his throat into the microphone. All eyes turned toward the floor of the gym, including Spencer's.

"We'd like to welcome our student body to the assembly. The last few months of school are going to be the best months. Not that the preceding months has been bad—but, well—" Principal Ackerman cleared his throat again, shoving wire glasses up his nose. "We intend to send our seniors out with a bang."

Applause roared through the room. All around her boys high-fived each other. Jennifer looked for John's dark hair.

"Some of our end-of-the-year activities I want to remind you of are the upcoming Save Our Water fundraiser. It's a waterless carwash sponsored by the Ecology club. It will be this Friday in the parking lot of the Purple Turtle, so everybody bring your vehicles down."

"How do you wash a car without water?" Spencer

mumbled. "I got bird crap on my hood that's, like, petrified."

Alex slugged Cort's deltoid. "I've seen this before, dude. They use spit. I swear."

"Seriously?"

"In three weeks," Principal Ackerman continued, again pushing his walnut-sized gold specs up. "We have our drama department's production of Romeo and Juliet." The entire room erupted into cat calls, screeching howls and whistles, rattling Jennifer's bones.

"I've heard it's going to be a great show." Principal Ackerman smiled up at her. "There's our girl. Jennifer Vienvu is Juliet." He let the applause die down before he continued. "And John...where's John Michaels? Ah. There he is. John plays Romeo." Nothing compared to the thunderous noise that rocked the inside of the building after John's name was spoken. As if the walls themselves strained to bow.

When John appeared down on the floor, every foot pounded into the bleachers. The chant of his name began. Jennifer hadn't seen him when they took their seats. She figured he was hiding off to the side of the bleachers just waiting for this moment. Over the rioting noise, guys and girls shouted to him.

"We love you John!"

"You're a sexy beast!"

"You rock, John!"

"Dude!"

John emerged with both hands clasped humbly and a grin on his face. He stood next to Principal Ackerman, himself caught in applause. *Jeez, what is this, the John Michaels show?*

Jennifer stopped clapping.

Principal Ackerman slid an arm around John's shoulder. "You can stay right here, John." Again the room screeched.

Jennifer sat upright. Did John *have* to look so adorably uncomfortable?

Nonchalantly, she glanced around. Most of the girls leaned forward as if at any moment they might spring from the bleachers and land at John's feet. She rolled her eyes.

"Thanks to our student body president." Principal Ackerman waved up the petite form of Ashley Torsau who'd hidden wherever John had hidden. Politely, John stepped aside. Ashley crossed the floor to the podium and Principal Ackerman. John's respectful acknowledgement of Ashley engaged the entire audience in another round of applause though this one much less enthusiastic. Jennifer felt bad for Ashley. Though she was well liked and well known, indeed those qualities had gotten her elected as student body president she couldn't hold a candle to John. She knew it and so did every body else.

And then there was John. John Michaels who ran for student body vice president on a whim, without even pinning up one poster or handing out a flyer to garner the winning votes that put him in office.

"Thanks to Ashley and John and the rest of student council, we have a surprise for the student body." Principal Ackerman let the silence bubble for a minute. "These two have single-handedly found a sponsor who will quadruple the proceeds earned from the play so the school can purchase new seats for the auditorium with the funds."

Again the room erupted into applause. Jennifer kept her narrowed eyes on John. He bowed his dark head of hair. He looked so angelic with those downcast lashes she almost puked. He wore humility well, she thought wryly. He wore everything well.

"You guys rock!" somebody shouted.

Principal Ackerman held his hand up to quiet the crowd. "We could use new seats. This means we need to have the biggest attendance to the play in the school's history. Come, and bring everyone you know. And then come again."

Reality hit Jennifer like a slap in the face. Everyone in this room would see her and John kiss. She sat perfectly still. Around her, students broke out into laughter and talk. She tried to swallow the knot in her throat, but it remained lodged there. The joke was on her. Her inexperience would be as obvious as the lie she started out of spite.

Rachel leaned close. "You're going to be in the spotlight, hon."

Jennifer watched John. Her heart floundered in fear. *I'll bet John could care less that the whole world is going to watch us. He's probably glad, knowing I'll look stupid.*

He looked out over the audience and she shrunk from his sweeping gaze. Normally, she took every opportunity to show herself in a desirable situation. Here she sat, surrounded by some of the hottest guys in school. The perfect op.

She turned to Spencer and Hugh, Alex and Cort. The boys' boredom instantly perked to interest when she flashed a smile. "Which one of you guys is the best kisser?"

FIVE

Kissing lessons. Who'd have thought?

Jennifer shook now as she walked the long hall to the stage after her chat with Alex Jesperson. When she posed the question of who was the best kisser, it didn't surprise her that all of the guys' hands had gone up. But it was Alex who won the coin toss. Spencer insisted on a toss for fairness.

Kissing lessons, coin tosses. Absurd. Jennifer almost laughed, but she shook too hard. It was pretty bad when you only locked lips because you were playing a character in a play. It was worse to *ask* someone to teach you how to kiss.

She opened the door to the drama room and found it empty.

Everybody was already on stage. She checked her watch. She loved the pink band with the fake diamonds surrounding the pearly face but she hated that the dumb thing was slow. This wasn't the first time this had happened, and she knew Chip knew it, too.

Piles of clothes were strewn everywhere. She remembered Chip mentioning they might try out costumes next rehearsal. She looked around for hers. Hanging on the movable garment rack were six colorful, long dresses. A big, white piece of paper was pinned to the sleeve of a purple gown with gauzy sleeves.

Jenn,

This is the dress you should put on first. If you're reading this note, you're late.

Chip

Jennifer crunched the note between nervous hands and pulled the dress from the hanger. It was dense as a wool blanket. She started to undress, carefully making a pile of clothes on the nearest chair. The room was oddly empty sounding for a place usually pulsing with energy. She caught the heavy scent of rancid body odor in the dress as she unzipped it.

Suddenly the door swung open. One hand flew to cover her bra, the other to cover her panties and she screeched.

John.

"I'm in here!" She reached for the dress, knocking the pile of clothes and the purple costume to the floor.

"Jenn? Sorry."

John shut the door. Furious, embarrassed, she yanked the dress on. "Can't you knock first?" she screamed.

Both sleeves slid up her arms and she wriggled into the bodice, realizing the garment was cut low, that it left her breasts looking like halves of white peaches. She also realized that there was no way her arms were going to suddenly lengthen, enabling her to zip the back up. She let out sigh.

Lifting the heavy skirts with one hand, she crossed to the mirror. Her eyes widened. *There is no way I am going to wear this thing.*

I look like a wench.

Turning, she took in the whole dress. It was flattering enough, if big skirts and full hips was what you liked.

It's a costume, get over it.

Still, every time she faced the mirror her eyes went directly to her chest. The way the bodice snugged created a deep line between her breasts she'd never had there before. She stared, fascinated. It looked... feminine. It looked—dared she think the word—tempting. She'd have to be careful when she bent over or she'd show the audience more than her acting talent during the play.

What will John think of the dress? Will he think I look...tempting? A pleasant shudder wove through her. There was no time to look for the shoes Taunia had set aside. Barefoot, she lifted the long skirts and ran out the door.

The stage still smelled faintly of paint, though the scent muddled in the mustiness of the costumes everyone was wore. She heard dialogue from one of the scenes and flew through the wings then remembered that her backside was exposed. She hoped her bra was clean. Was she wearing the pink one or the one with the turquoise and red flowers?

"Hey." John's whisper. He was nearly hidden in the long black drapes hanging randomly backstage.

She stopped. Her face heated. The colors in his eyes deepened as he swept her from head to toe. "Wow."

She thought the same of him. His wild dark hair was striking against the autumn colors in his clothing. His golden skin set darker against the blousy white shirt underneath an ornately beaded vest in rich jewel tones. Though she'd seen his legs plenty of times at the pool, when he wore shorts, while mowing his lawn his legs looked boyishly cute in hunter green tights now. She squelched a laugh. "Are those tights?"

He shifted. "Shut up, will ya?"

"Oh." The draft on her back had her turning her spine toward him. "Could you do me?"

"Excuse me?"

She shot him a grin. "Hurry. Chip's gonna kill me."

"You're always late, Vien."

"It's my watch."

"Hmm."

He gently eased the zipper up. She went still. A line of heat traced from the bottom of the zipper all the way to the top. When he finished, she took a deep breath and turned. His dark brows were cinched over eyes now serious. "Thank you," she said.

"No problem."

As she turned to go to the stage, he stopped her with a light touch to her elbow.

"Jenn?"

"Yeah?"

"Sorry about earlier. I was—I didn't think anybody was in there."

She almost reminded him it wasn't the first time he'd caught her nearly butt-naked. But the look on his face

and the warm thickness in the air between them had
her wondering if he already remembered. Neighbors.
Windows. Oops.

Shrugging made her feel better, like the incident
was nothing. But it was. It was a naked dream come to
life. And she was always the one naked.

He'd never remember his lines now. His brain
was branded with the stark image of Jennifer in her
underwear. The flash of vision hadn't missed a thing and
he cleared his throat as a fast, hot surge jammed his
system. No, he'd pretty much seen it all.

He smiled.

Sweat popped out around his neck, under his arms.
Heat flushed him from head to toe. It was hot enough
on stage. He didn't need to think about Jennifer in her
underwear. He lifted his tunic away from his body so air
cooled his steaming skin. John stayed in the fringes of
the stage watching and his gaze found her and only her.
Juliet talked to her mother, Lady Capulet, and her nurse
trying to convince them that her love was justified, even if
that love was forbidden.

John filled with awe. Jennifer was amazing. Every
line flowed with emotion and passion. Her moves weren't
staged but completely natural. The way the lights
glistened off her pale hair was like the sun and moon
had become one. No one had eyes the color of blue
diamonds like she did. So multi-faceted, he had to look
long and hard to believe they were real, and even then,
that wasn't enough.

At first he was afraid he might not be able to match her performance. She'd been doing this theater stuff way longer than he had. He'd even been to some of her plays over the years. He'd watched her abilities grow. Now she was just plain awesome.

He didn't back down from the challenge because if he worked hard enough he could do it. None of it came naturally for him. Before he'd set one foot at a rehearsal he spent hours in front of mirrors practicing.

Jennifer simply walked onto the stage and *was* Juliet.

The kiss was coming and his heart tripped thinking about it. He almost kissed her last night. He wanted to. It was a kick, seeing her all worried. But deep inside, something he'd never felt before happened when her eyes teared. Something that made him want to hug her. More than that even. He wanted to comfort her.

He'd make sure the kiss they shared tonight was better than the last one. He never thought much about kissing. He thought it just happened, that nature took its course and then it was what it was. He wondered if more was expected of him. He scanned the faces of those in the room, most with their eyes on the action. A handful of eyes met his, girls mostly.

They'd all watch him kiss Jennifer.

Movement caught his eye. In the faded light shining on the front rows of seats, Alex Jesperson moseyed down the aisle. The football player's body might have been moseying but John recognized the intense stare on the guy's face. Intensely focused on...John followed Alex's heavy gaze right to Jennifer. He looked from Jennifer to Alex.

No way.

The guy smiled and sat all husky and jock-like, propping his big feet on the seat in front of him. The sight grated at John like cleats on bare flesh. Jennifer hadn't noticed Alex's entrance since she was too focused on the scene. Almost time for the kiss. John relished his chance. It wasn't that he didn't like Alex. There wasn't anybody at school he couldn't hang with and he'd hung with Alex and Spencer and their friends before. But he had more than the play riding on this production.

John didn't care why Alex was there. Whatever he had to do, he'd do. And right now, he had to make this kiss so hot that Jennifer melted into the floor.

Chip called a five-minute break. Most of the actors fanned themselves with their hands. Nobody dared moan about the heat, about how heavy and uncomfortable the rented, perfectly accurate renaissance costumes were. Chip was a perfectionist down to the finest detail: no fingernail polish for the ladies, no bleach-tipped hair for the guys and absolutely no jewelry or tat on any visible body part. Only Andrew had whined about that, knowing he'd have to put pancake makeup over the small tattoo of snakes sitting like a necklace around the base of his throat.

Jennifer wanted to unzip her dress and cool off but since that wasn't possible she walked to the edge of the stage where lights dropped off into darkness. Maybe it wasn't as hot there as it was center stage.

She saw Alex. He sent a studly wave and mouthed, "Hey."

Jennifer looked around to see who he was waving at. When it was clear it was her he was scamming, her face scrunched. To make sure he didn't blow the lid off their secret pact she went to him, holding her skirt up as she walked.

"Hey." Grinning big, he sat forward. His eyes sparkled with something Jennifer didn't recognize but looked on the edge of nasty. "You look good up there." His low voice dropped to the gutter.

"Thanks." She glanced over her shoulder at the stage. The sets were wonderfully detailed down to faux brick walls. The lattice John climbed to her balcony was brand new. He'd be safe on it, even if he did have to dodge a hedge of plastic red roses.

She searched for him and found him on stage standing with Chip, the two talking.

"So, what are you doing here?" She turned back around to Alex.

"I thought we could, you know, after the practice. Want to?"

Her heart thumped. "Uh. Well. I'm not sure how long we'll go. It gets late sometimes."

Alex reached out and looped some of her hair in his fingertips. A lazy grin spread across his face. "Can't wait."

Jennifer stiffened. *Uh-oh. What have I done? Brought a monster to life? No, Alex isn't really a monster. He's a football player, heavy emphasis on the player.* "I'll probably be really tired after," she explained. "Really tired."

He still had her hair in his fingers, wasn't letting go. "I'll wake you up."

As casually as she could, she eased back. Her hair

fell to the side of her face. Chip announced the five-minute break was over and relief coursed through her. "I have to go."

Alex sat back in the chair, as if his butt was rooted. "I'll be right here."

"Oh—okay."

Jennifer wrung her hands as she walked back to the stage. The heat of every curious eye in the auditorium pricked her in the back. Snaky whispers snuck in the air. Her gaze fell directly on John. His gaze bore into hers.

"Let's take it from scene twenty," Chip announced. "John. Jenn."

The stage cleared. Because scene twenty was the scene where they kissed, none of the cast disappeared backstage; they eagerly found seats in the auditorium.

" 'Kay you guys, we'll start whenever you're ready," Chip called, his voice fading as he walked to the rear of the theater. "People, take your seats, we're almost out of time."

John only briefly looked down at the tape marking the spot on the dark wood floor. His eyes lifted to Jennifer's. Raw determination set firmly in his jaw, fired bright colors in his eyes. Jennifer took in a deep breath. It wasn't enough. She couldn't think of her line.

The room was quiet as a tomb.

"Jenn?" Chip asked.

Her entire body flushed. "I'm ready." Then she made herself walk to her starting mark.

John began. *"With love's light wings did I o'erperch these walls, for stony limits cannot hold love out."*

Intensity snapped in the hot air around John. Gold flecks in his eyes lit to fiery amber. Muscles in his arms and body flexed and moved with urgency. Jennifer almost lost her train of thought. She had to switch gears fast. She forgot the bodies to her right and the scent of paint evaporated. When the music crested, cuing them to kiss, her heart soared with the violins. He took her hands. Gently, he drew her toward him and the air was filled with everything wonderful and curious about him, past and present.

She wet her lips, looking at his as he spoke.

"Alack, there lies more peril in thine eye than twenty of their swords. Look thou but sweet, and I am proof against their enmity."

She took a breath and said, *"I would not for the world they saw thee here."*

"I have night's cloak to hide me from their eyes. And but thou love me, let them find me here. My life were better ended by their hate, than prorogued, wanting of thy love."

The colors in his eyes shifted, like a rainbow moved by the breeze. Silence surrounded them. His head dipped. She closed her eyes, eager to taste the soft sweetness of him again.

"We're out of time, guys," Chip's booming voice severed the silky silence.

Jennifer's eyes shot open, John's did the same. Both moved back, still joined at their hands by the poetic exchange of words. Chip ordered the house lights up over moans and complaints barking from the cast who felt gypped not getting to see the kiss.

"Sorry, guys." Chip held up both hands as he quickly strode to the front of the stage, clipboard tucked under his arm. "But I've had a few complaints from parents who will remain nameless about rehearsals going too late."

Another round of groaning followed, snapped by accusations and finger pointing as the group tried to figure out whose parents snitched. Chip hoisted himself onto the lip of the stage. Jennifer expected John to let go of her hands. His face shadowed with something she'd not seen since they were much younger, when one day she chose to play with a new girl in the neighborhood over him.

When he finally let go, she crossed her arms over her chest, hiding her empty hands and watched him move across the stage to Chip.

SIX

There was no way to get out of it. Now Alex was following her home, his loud, fire engine-red truck with its diesel engine chugging behind her bright yellow VW like a roaring dragon after a baby duck.

As awkward went this moment, the next few moments, or however long they'd be at it, would rate as her most memorable. Jennifer really didn't have any idea what to expect, having only kissed on stage that once.

Her parent's kissed everywhere, in the car, at the mall, in restaurants. She'd seen kids kiss at school, in the hall, before class, on the grass at lunch. Just where did Alex intend to give her these kissing lessons?

She took her time parking in the driveway, even though she knew very well how to park the car. She powdered her chin and nose, looked at her scared eyes in her compact and then glanced in her rear-view mirror. Alex's big red truck sat idling in the street, its parking lights two dim embers of sin.

She swallowed.

She couldn't stay in the car all night. Truthfully, she hadn't thought ahead. How would she explain to her parents the red truck parked out front with windows that just might get steamy?

She got out of the car clutching her backpack to her chest like a shield. Alex was halfway up the driveway, his muscular form striding casually, confidently. Jennifer thought she must look like a nerdy third-string player readying to be tackled.

They stood facing each other in the unseasonably bitter cold air of the spring night.

"So." Alex shrugged, smiled. "How about we get in my truck? It's warm."

Biting her lip, Jennifer nodded. "Okay. Sure." Then she looked over her shoulder at her house, lights glowing from random windows. Her mother would come out, suspicious of any car she didn't recognize, and Alex Jesperson's red truck had not been a regular in the neighborhood.

"Just let me take my stuff inside," she told him.

The house was warm and smelled of garlic and Italian sauce. The warmth didn't take away the chill that lying caused her. She dropped her backpack in a chair in the front room. "Mom?"

"In here."

Jennifer followed the sound of her mother's voice and found her family around the kitchen table with two steaming pizzas, half devoured, in the center. Four liters of root beer were nearly empty. Her brother Parker had one liter possessively tucked in the crook of his arm. His right hand held a floppy triangle of pepperoni pizza at his eager mouth. He grunted. Little Amber reached for her liter bottle with two greasy hands. She stopped when she saw Jennifer, her red-smeared lips breaking into a smile. "Jefer!"

"Hey." The greeting warmed Jennifer. A sudden sadness came over her, like she was about to give something of her innocence away. She took Amber's pizza-greased face in both of her hands and squeezed, willing the sadness inside to leave. It was only a kiss, she reminded herself. And she was doing this for a reason, to be able to deliver a believable kiss on stage.

"You going to eat?" her dad asked.

"Nah." Jennifer quickly headed back to the front door. Her stomach was in jumbles and she didn't want to have garlic-breath. "I've got to do some studying. I'll be back. Oh." She stopped, tried to appear casual. "We'll be studying out front."

"In this weather?" Her mother craned her neck to look outside the bay window into the back yard at the trembling trees. "It's freezing."

"I know. We'll be in the truck."

Both of her parents stopped chewing and looked at her, their cheeks bulging with food. Her father swallowed. "Truck?"

"We?"

"Yeah. I just didn't want you to be worried when you saw the red truck and, you know, didn't know whose it was." She turned.

"Whose truck?"

Jennifer stopped. "Alex Jesperson."

Her parents exchanged looks of surprise. "Alex Jesperson, the football player Alex Jesperson?" her mother asked.

"That's him."

"You know him?" she asked.

Jennifer shrugged. *I'm going to know him a lot better in a few minutes.* The very idea knotted her stomach. "Yeah. He needs some help in English."

Her dad got back to eating, satisfied with the

explanation. "Most football players can't read their way across a football field."

But her mother wasn't convinced. Skepticism crossed her face. "Well..." Her mother's heavy pause was interrupted by Amber's whine for another liter of soda. "It's nice that you can help him."

Jennifer closed the front door with a quaking heart. Standing on the porch, she looked at the shiny truck. Alex sent her a friendly wave from inside the cab, then his fingers curled, beckoning.

Cold nipped at her now that she was outside, and she started toward the truck. She glanced at John's house, then down the street. Not seeing his car in the driveway had her wondering where he was, if he'd stayed after rehearsal to help Chip, something he was known to do.

Candy-coated thoughts of John flooded her. His face and all of its familiar expressions flashed into her mind. Her whole body yearned for the ease of being with him as she approached the unknown.

Alex leaned over the long stretch of front seat and opened the door for her. Why did she feel like she stood in front of the gaping jaws of a shark?

He patted the seat with a smile. "Come on in."

"Wow." Jennifer pulled herself up and into the cab, but her foot slipped. "You need to be a mountain climber to get into this thing."

Alex laughed. Reaching over, his fingers wrapped tight around her upper arms and he drew her to him. Jennifer's laugh fluttered out. She lay on her stomach the full length of the seat, her head perched in his lap. She looked up at him.

He grinned.

Then he helped her sit up.

Jennifer cleared her throat and pressed her rigid spine into the back of the seat. The heater blasted warm air in her face. She felt like she was in a car commercial with a perpetual wind blowing her hair. Hard rock music pounded from speakers. She liked the band well enough, but didn't think the tune particularly romantic.

"You wanna close the door?" Alex asked, stretching out his long arm along the back of the seat.

"Oh. Sure." She slammed it shut and the thud closed everything around them into a box. In that instant, she realized where she was and exactly what was going to happen.

Alex looked amazingly comfortable and at ease, she thought, half annoyed. *He's no doubt done this hundreds, if not, zillions of times.* He was the lion, she was the cat. Though they were the same species, there was a world of difference between them.

For a long while, they looked at each other. Finally, Alex shifted, reaching his long, bulging arm out toward her. She shrunk against the door. He smiled. "Don't be scared, Jenn. It's okay." His meaty palm wrapped around her bicep and he pulled. The next thing she knew, she slid across the seat until she was snugged up to his side. "There," he said, wrapping his arm around her. "Or are you just acting scared, you know, to get me hot."

Her breath raced in and out. *Nope, this is real.* She looked at his face, so near she could count the blonde stubble like sand across his jaw. His light eyes sparkled. She'd never noticed that his lips were wide and full, pulled back now in another lazy grin.

"Just relax," he told her.

"Okay," she said, but the words warbled out.

"You're too tense. I feel it." He tugged her close. "Let go."

"O-Okay," she repeated, and went stiffer.

He took her chin in his fingers and lifted her mouth up, looking at it. "You have great lips."

"I do?"

Nodding, his gaze sharpened. "Great lips." She watched his mouth descend to hers and then she said, "What makes lips great?"

He seemed in a daze for a few seconds. "Uh, well. I don't know." His eyes dropped back to her mouth. "Supple. Ample. Kissable." His eyes darkened, his fingers dug at her shoulder. "Sexy."

This time he dove for her mouth. At first, she backed her neck into the crook of his arm. But his lips had adhered to hers. The hardened plane of his chest pressed her into the seat. The heater turned into an inferno. She sweat. His lips were warm, wet. Not soft like John's, but slippery, moving over her mouth, tugging and nipping. She winced, but he swallowed it. She'd heard about tongues, but teeth? Strangely, the hard enamel of his teeth against the tenderness of her mouth sent a brilliant strain through her.

"Put your arms around my neck," he whispered. She did. Their faces were so close, his was a blur. He took only a moment to look into her eyes before his eyes shifted down to her mouth with another eager look. She wondered if he was going to kiss her again.

"Am I doing it right?" she asked.

He barely nodded before inching toward her. "Oh,

yeah." Then his mouth was hot on hers again, shooting heat in fast, riveting sparks everywhere inside of her.

His arms wove around her, and he eased her back so they were lying down on the bench. Halfway down, Jennifer opened her eyes. His were closed, his light lashes fluttering against his cheekbones. Strange. But then what did she expect? To find him with his eyes open?

The weight of his football-player body smashing her caused her lungs to feel like two balloons, slowly being compressed. She turned her head, searching for air but his mouth followed hers. A little squeak erupted in the back of her throat. He went still. He lifted up, looking down at her. "You okay?"

She gulped in air, nodded. That heavy-lidded look meant he was going to dive for more; so she pressed her palms to his shoulders. "Uh, can we take a little break?"

He froze, hanging over the full length of her. He let out a sigh and nodded as he sat upright, running his hands over his face.

Jennifer scrambled up and decided then that the prostrate position was not for her, at least not at this moment in time, with this particular guy. And she wasn't sure she was learning anything. Wasn't there more to kissing than this? Technique or something?

"So," she began casually tucking a stray hair behind her ear, "Is there anything I need to know? I mean, you know, about doing it?"

Alex's eyes hooded. Extending his arm once again behind her, he shook his head. "You're doing fine to me."

But I don't know what I'm doing, she thought miserably. Surely, as with anything else, this thing can be taught. She figured he must have seen her dismay, because he said, "Okay, look. Keep your lips moist, but not too wet. And parted. Nobody kisses with their mouths closed, that's only in the black and whites."

"Black and whites?"

"Yeah, the old movies." He went silent then, staring at her mouth as if it was something edible and he was ready for a snack. The muscles in his arm shifted, coiled around her shoulder and he brought her over for more.

"You worry too much," he said with an amused smile. He lowered his head and kissed her again.

She made herself relax against him. Kissing Alex wasn't as enjoyable as it was with John. Alex's cologne was too musky, filling her nostrils with a scent that almost desensitized her nose. He told her to keep her lips moist, but his bordered on slobbery. Every time he pulled back the air hit wet and she felt like she needed a napkin or her sleeve.

Still, the way his body moved, his hands stroked, it was obvious he was enjoying himself. She liked knowing that. The gentle pressure he exerted against her only became more urgent as minutes ticked by, as if he was forced by a power he couldn't resist. It gave her a sense of feminine power she'd never felt before.

Amidst the euphoria, she heard the familiar clattering of John's engine out the window.

Alex's mouth moved like a fish's, opening and closing, opening and closing, and she wasn't sure what she was supposed to do in response. *Open—close? Stay closed?* When he moaned every nerve inside of her swayed with gratification. Alex made her feel things... things triumphant.

John's rattling engine slowed outside the red truck.

Jennifer heard it idle for a moment before it revved once and then died shortly thereafter.

When Alex's hands began to move, her eyes shot open. Alarms rang in her head. She wasn't ready to share any other part of herself with Alex and she wriggled away, quickly looking at the windows blocked by fog so dense tears of sweat dripped down them.

"What?" he croaked.

"I can't see."

He looked utterly confused. "See what? All the action's right here."

She sat as close to the door as she could, taking in a deep breath of moist, breathy air. "So, you think I can do it?"

"Oh, you can do it. Come back here." Leaning her direction, he grinned. The glittering in his eye was as obvious as a neon light outside a strip club. He wanted to kiss her again. With the power of the moment in her hand, she decided to try out her new skills and moved closer to him like a little girl leaning her face to an alluring flower she wanted to sniff but might hold a bee.

Alex seemed spellbound, captured. Jennifer delicately pressed her lips to his in a simple kiss that left him motionless.

She sighed happily at what she did to him. "Alex. Thanks." Then she opened the door and got out, taking one more opportunity to look at him, stretched out on the bench, eyes closed, his mouth poised and waiting.

Finally, he sat back, letting out a blustering sigh. "Whew. Later, Jenn."

She shut the door with a smile of newfound secrets.

Crossing the grass her steps crunched the iced

blades. Wind, weaving through the lacy leaves of the locust trees, seemed caught in applause, as if they, too, were pleased for her. She looked up into the black sky and stared at the sparkling stars. *Sparkling, like Alex's eyes.*

Her dreamy gaze came down from the sky, star by star until it reached the warm glow of John's window. She stopped. He was there. When he saw that she had finally discovered him, his shoulders twitched. Then he turned, vanished, and the room went dark.

SEVEN

"Man, what's up with you?" Justin trailed John toward the locker room after a sweaty sprint around the track. "If coach had been timing you, he'd have clocked you at half your record speed."

John shoved the double doors open. Younger, more easily impressed boys kept respectfully behind him in the march from the field, and now they slowed with caution. As captain of the track team, every other boy in the phys ed program at Pleasant View High School understood John held a title that reigned alongside football captain and basketball captain. His outstanding state scores had taken the track team to national competitions three years in a row, winning PVHS the title—something no other school team captain had accomplished. Because of his social status, when John Michaels walked through a room the crowd parted. Conversely, when John was angry, or anything less than the have-a-smile-and-a-hey-for-everyone, the crowd took notice.

John yanked his sweat-drenched tee shirt over his head and balled it between two tight fists, striding to his locker. Justin did the same. "So, what's up?" Justin persisted.

John wiped the sweat beading his face with the tee shirt and flipped the dial. "Nothing." He didn't want to talk to anybody, not even one of his friends, about what he witnessed last night.

The younger boys already in the locker room quieted. Most pretended they weren't listening. Those clueless stood and watched him.

"Dude, where should we hit for lunch?" Justin pulled open his own locker three doors down from John's.

Commotion at the entrance of the locker room had all the boys turning their attention to Alex Jesperson, coming in followed by half a dozen football players who'd shared the field with the track team during PE. They laughed and talked—about Jennifer. John's eyes sharpened on the group sauntering in, stripping on the way to their lockers.

"You scored better than an astronaut, dude." One of the beefy guys slapped a meaty palm on Alex's muscled back. "Going where no man has gone before."

The other players laughed and made a variety of cat calls. Alex lifted his burly arms upward in a gesture of victory. "It was sweet."

"I'll teach Jennifer how to kiss any time. Give her my number," somebody said.

"Stand in line, fat brain," another put in.

Alex shook his head. "She's mine, dudes. No, I'm serious. She's virgin territory. I like that."

"You have Amanda."

"You mean he's *had* Amanda." The guys ribbed each other.

"So?" Alex flung a towel over his shoulder. "This chick has wicked lips for a first-timer."

"That still blows me away." One guy shook his sweaty head. "Who'd have guessed the diva had never been kissed."

The muscles in John's stomach clenched. He loitered at his locker, trying to catch as much of the conversation he could, but this news shocked him. *Jenn, never been kissed?* His insides roiled with disappointment. Alex had kissed her.

Strapping white towels around their waists, the boys headed for the showers.

Steam fogged the open-area room. Towels were tossed on hooks just outside the wide opening and the boys filed in, still laughing and talking. John stole the shower next to Alex's. The two looked at each other and nodded before sticking their heads under streams of hot water.

"You hitting on Jennifer now?" John reached for soap.

Alex lifted his right arm and sudsed his armpit. "Yeah, you could say that."

Playing along with Alex was harder than playing Romeo. John's jaw was rock hard, but he faked a smile. "I thought you and Amanda were it."

Alex leaned his head back under the water then shook out his hair like a dog. "Hey, the more the merrier, you know?"

"Don't lie about it, man." One of Alex's friends stood in the next half-stall over. "You didn't go all the way. She's still a *virgin*."

"Not for long." Alex laughed, rubbing his slick chest with both hands. "She was hot for me. And I can make her hot again."

Anger bubbled like a volcano ready to blow inside of John. He thought he hit his limit last night when he saw the windows of Alex's red truck dense with the fog of lust.

He'd almost sent his fist through one.

Up until junior high school, John knew everything about Jennifer, including the kind of boys she liked. But then that was another girl, and he wasn't even sure if any part of her still lived inside of this Jennifer anymore. It didn't matter. Something inside of him despised Alex for having done something with Jennifer that he had foolishly hoped to do.

Kissing her on stage didn't count.

Whatever happened in that truck, Jennifer had concurred, and the very idea churned John's gut with disappointment. And regret. He twisted off the water and rubbed his hands hard down his face. Then he reached for his towel.

Jennifer had only five minutes to get to English. She had to find Rachel. Weaving in and around sauntering students ignorant of the short time between bells, she spotted Rachel in the crowded hall. Her head was thrown back in a laugh and her dark, ruler-straight hair fell dramatically down her back. She was surrounded by guys, none of which was Alex, thankfully. Because it was Alex Jennifer needed to talk about.

The boys opened the tight circle for her and Jennifer slipped in with a smile. "Hey."

She was greeted with respectful nods, a couple of "Hey's", and a pat to her arm. Maybe she was just imagining it, but they all looked as if they were happy for her. Like she just won the lotto.

"We'll catch you later, Rache," Todd said before leaving. When he shrugged away, the other boys followed.

Rachel turned, flipped her dark hair over her shoulder and started the walk to her next class with Jennifer. "So," she said, waiting.

"So." Jennifer began. Memories of the night before cast a dreamy haze over her brain. "It was great."

"Yeah, Alex is pretty hot."

"He told me I was—" Jennifer looked around before leaning into Rachel, lowering her voice, "he told me I was fine."

"So you're okay with it all now, right? You feel like you can deliver?"

Jennifer nodded. "I wonder if Alex will call me. He's kinda cute."

"Whoa." Rachel stopped, put a hand on Jennifer's shoulder. "Wait a minute. You've never said one word about Alex before."

"Because we hadn't kissed each other before."

"You've got it all wrong, hon. Way wrong." Rachel tugged Jennifer to a corner of the hall as bodies rushed by. The bell shrilled in their ears but Rachel ignored it, her face tight to Jennifer's. "Nothing happened last night, did it? I mean, you just kissed, right?"

"Yes."

Rachel relaxed. "Good. For a second you had me worried."

"Why?"

"You sounded like you *like* Alex."

"I do like Alex."

"But not *that* way."

"Why not *that* way? I mean, we kissed last night.
It was—"

"Jenn." Rachel squared her shoulders and looked
her in the eye. "It was FWB, nothing more. He's, like,
dating Amanda Flanders."

Jennifer's heart took a pinch. "You're right. I've seen
them together."

Rachel flipped her hair back again and started
off to class. "Making out is a sport to most guys, nothing
more—just for the fun of it."

Any lingering sense of power and euphoria Jennifer
had from the night before was squashed under the
truthful weight of Rachel's words. Rachel was right; she'd
sat around and discussed this very topic before, only it
had never affected her directly so she hadn't given it
much thought. Until now.

Too disappointed to say anything more, she
covered disillusionment with a fake smile. But she was
wounded inside. What did she expect? It was a tutoring
lesson, nothing more.

"Have you and Alex...ever?" she asked.

"A long time ago. It was nothing. Hey, I'll see you
after class. Sanderson already hates my guts. Now I'll
have to talk him out of another tardy."

Rachel half-jogged the other direction, her dark hair
flying behind her.

Emptiness was everywhere, in the hollow hall, inside
Jennifer's chest. She thought what happened between
her and Alex was important, tutoring lesson or not. Kissing
was intimate. Kissing should be special. Now she felt
stupid.

She glanced at her watch, it was fifteen minutes

slow. She was fifteen minutes late. For once she didn't want to correct the hands on the dial of her watch, as if just looking at them could take everything back.

You couldn't sneak unnoticed into a class like Ms. Tingey's. She stood at the front of the room, in the middle of discussing *Pride and Prejudice*. As usual, she had a lively discussion going; hands were up, voices raised. A smile was across her face.

Jennifer slid in. She shot Ms. Tingey an apologetic shrug and crossed to her desk on the opposite side of the room. Of course, she had to pass directly in front of John.

Ms. Tingey didn't give out tardies unless you were an obvious idiot who made no effort to be on time.

Jennifer reached into her backpack for her copy of the book. Her eyes were on Ms. Tingey, but she saw John out of the corner of her eye, slightly turned her direction.

I have nothing to be ashamed of she told herself, but wondered why meeting his gaze proved difficult. She dug for a pen and stuck it between her teeth, primly crossing her legs before smiling at the few faces waiting for her notice.

To prove it, she chanced a look at John. Normally, his opal eyes danced with playfulness and confidence. Today they were stormy, locked on hers from across the room.

With one blink, she looked back at Ms.Tingey, ignoring him. But the pleasant trembling his look caused inside of her stomach remained.

"Let's connect the chapter we just read to our lives.

Anybody?"

A guy in the front row slumped forward in his desk. "I don't connect with it at all."

"Isn't that the chapter where Kitten runs off and gets hooked up?" Freddy leaned back in a stretch.

"Her name's Lydia," Jessica sneered from behind him. "But don't get hung up on details."

The class erupted in laughter—until John spoke out, slapping the room with silence. "I think it's interesting that Lydia is so anxious to experience life that she's willing to run off with some low-life all because he's got a title and big biceps."

Miss Tingey added, "Excellent observation."

"Well," Jennifer's blood began to simmer. "I think it's really sad that her family, her sisters, her *friends* overshadowed her so that she felt like she had to make a name for herself."

"Oh, she made a name for herself," John piped with a bite of sarcasm.

Freddy laughed. "Yeah—skank."

A little laughter trickled in the room, but the steam building sucked it away in a fast breath.

"Well." Jennifer tucked her hair behind her ears and re-crossed her legs. "I've finished the rest of the book, and it seems to me that obviously Lydia thought there'd be more to the relationship. It's the guy who used her."

"My point exactly," John said. "Why should someone with no experience in something trust someone they don't know anything about?"

"That wasn't your point," Jennifer snapped. "Your point was you think it's wrong for any girl to go with someone you think is not socially acceptable. Lydia was being led by her heart."

"She'd have been better off being led by her head."

"Like guys always think with their heads?"

"I know I don't." Freddy added and the boys let out clipped laughs before dropping into silence again.

"Lydia was being selfish," John continued as if Freddy hadn't said anything. "She shamed her family and her *friends*"

"Her *friends* had no right to be ashamed of her. She was doing what she had to do."

"That's bull."

"Oh, wait, you're right," Jennifer replied sharply. "She didn't have to do it. She *wanted* to."

"Okay." Miss Tingey rubbed her hands together. "Let's change the discussion. Let's get into Elizabeth and Mr. Darcy's relationship."

Jessica raised her hand and Miss Tingey looked noticeably relaxed that the girl was contributing. "They both love each other but are," she lifted her fingers and made the sign of quotations, "'too proud' to admit it."

It infuriated Jennifer that John looked ready to fight. *Fine, let's go a few more rounds.*

"Well, actually," John said first, "at this point in the story—sorry, Ms. Tingey, but I've finished the book, too. At this point, Mr. Darcy has already asked her to marry him. It's Elizabeth who's got the pride issue."

"If Mr. Darcy didn't act so egotistical at the beginning of the story," Jennifer shot at him, "treating her like she's some hangnail on his finger, then there wouldn't be a problem."

"I thought you said you finished the story," John

shot back. "Mr. Darcy ends up saving her and her family's reputation."

"I know that. But thanks for spoiling the ending for everyone who hasn't finished."

"Okay." This time Miss Tingey was more firm. "I think we all agree Mr. Darcy turns out to be the classic romantic literary hero."

Jennifer rolled her eyes. "Why is it always the guys in these books come out as heroes?"

The girls voiced their agreement, but the boys began to tease them.

"In Jane Austin's time," John started, his voice loud enough to quiet the teasing, "showing a strong woman as a leading character was progressive." He looked right at Miss Tingey with that air of cool confidence that caused everyone else to devotedly agree. Then he faced the class. "But we all know that chicks dig it when guys save the day."

John's palm met Freddy's in a slap of approval. The guys in the laughed out in agreement. Most of the girls blushed and smiled at the comment, knowing that whatever John said, was. Except Jennifer. She glared at him and muttered, "Somebody has a Superman complex."

EIGHT

Chip and Principal Ackerman thought it was a great idea if the cast had a contest. Whoever sold the most tickets to the play got a day off of school with an excused absence. At her locker, Jennifer changed books for class. She noticed a disruption down the hall by John's locker. It was a joke that they were even having this contest.

Every one knew John would win.

She slammed her locker shut and started to walk toward the bubble surrounding him. He'd been such a jerk in Tingey's class; she only wished she could make him look like an idiot in front these worshipping lemmings.

His electric smile blasted through the wiggling bodies in the crowd. Her heart skipped whether she wanted it to her not. His dark hair was ruffled and messy, like he'd just come in from the wind, and his eyes were set ablaze against the white tee shirt he wore.

"I didn't get your name," he said, leaning down so he could talk to a petite girl in the group. He wrote something in his ticket book, smiled that brilliant smile, and handed the girl a ticket. "Here. Thanks, Gretchen. See you at the show."

Gretchen and her friends squeezed out of the crowd, glowing like they'd just gotten autographs from Johnny Depp.

"How many do you want, Chris?" John slapped palms with a guy everybody called "Runt." Runt was over six feet but didn't play basketball because he was gangly and as uncoordinated as a giraffe on drugs. His face looked like it had been caught in a waffle iron. No one knew how Chris Sorenson had gotten the scars, but the hideous markings left him with few friends.

Long before John became *John*, he was kind to Runt. Jennifer remembered seeing Chris at the Michaels' house. John and Runt hanging in the back yard as John mowed the lawn, the two of them mulling around the annual Strawberry Days carnival every June. And when they went to dances, he always made sure Runt didn't stay pressed against a dark wall somewhere.

It impressed Jennifer that, even now, when everything beautiful and socially acceptable was available to John, he took time with Runt.

"If you need a ride that night, let me know." John ripped a ticket and handed it to Runt. Runt nodded and went on his way.

"Is it true you kiss Juliet in the play?" a girl asked. John looked up from writing out another receipt and gave a quick nod.

"It is."

The girl looked at her friends with a sparkling grin. "How many times?" she asked.

John's cheeks flushed. Jennifer felt her own do the same. "Guess you'll have to come and see for yourself."

"Oh, I'll be there." The girl handed John her money. John took it and stole another glance down the hall where Runt had gone.

"I'm Kimmy," the girl said. Her friends rattled off their

names.

John gave each of them an acknowledging nod. "You're all coming to the play, right?"

Of course they were.

Jennifer let out a sigh. Her allotment of tickets sat in her pocket. She'd never sell all of them.

After the girls left, John happened to see her. He didn't smile, rather sent another sharp look like the ones he'd sent her in Miss Tingey's class. She wanted to say something mean, something to tear him down a notch. But she couldn't find it in her heart, beating faster now that he'd pinned her with that opal gaze.

"John." Mr. Daniels, the Western Civilization teacher, was heading toward him and John finally looked away. John smiled and extended a hand to him.

"Hey, Mr. Daniels. What can I do for you?"

"I could use your help for a minute in my classroom." The slightly-hunched teacher turned back around and started down the hall the same way he had just come. John glanced at his watch before he took off after him. "Hear you've got tickets to the play." Mr. Daniels dug into his front pocket and produced a brown, leather wallet.

"I sure do, sir."

"Give me six. I'll bring the fam."

"You have four kids? Wow." John scribbled onto his ticket book and followed Mr. Daniels. Jennifer went on to her next class.

John pulled into his driveway and glanced at the Vienvu's house. Nagging curiosity still pestered him. His mind wouldn't stop flashing images of the red truck, the steamy windows, the locker room brag session he'd heard from Alex. Did Jennifer know she was shower-room fodder? She'd hate it.

He looked at his watch. There wasn't a lot of time before he had to be back at school for the final dress rehearsal. He had time for dinner and that was all. Any studying would have to be squeezed in between scenes.

Inside the house, John smelled basil, garlic and onions. His mother had made his favorite meal— lasagna. She never made it unless they were having guests, the huge pan she baked it in made enough for two families. He went directly to the kitchen and found her fussing over a large bowl filled with colorful greens.

"John. What happened to you today?"

He headed for the refrigerator. "What do you mean?"

"I mean you forgot Elise's driving test appointment."

John's teeth grazed his lower lip. A wave of guilt drowned him. "Lasagna?" He wanted to change the subject. "Who's coming over for dinner?" He took out the orange juice carton and drank.

"Get a glass."

"Ah." He stuck the carton back in the refrigerator with sigh.

"The Vienvu's."

John's hand froze on the handle of the refrigerator door. "Tonight?"

"Right now." His mother reached for salt and pepper.

John looked at his watch. "Is Dad home?"

Janice Michaels nodded toward the hall. That

meant his father was in his office, working. It also meant his dad was under pressure. He never brought his work home unless things weren't going well at the office.

"He wasn't happy about having to take Elise," his mother warned.

He could avert a face-to-face meeting with his dad, he'd done it before. But that was cowardly and his dad would call him on it. There was something to being the first to say *sorry*. John figured it would put this screwy chess game of apology at checkmate, in his favor.

He ventured down the dark hall to the open door of the office and peered in. His dad sat over the desk, deep into a pile of paperwork. John hesitated before clearing his throat. His dad's dark head swung up. A small wave was all his dad granted him before he was back at work again.

John waited a moment longer, not sure if he'd be called in and yelled at because he'd missed Elise's appointment. Heavy tension kept his father glued to his work. John wished there was something he could do to help, but he knew very little about security investing. All he knew was that when the stock market went up and down, his dad's moods often followed.

John was glad the Vienvu's were coming for dinner. If anybody could get his dad out of a mood rut, it was Randy Vienvu. The two men were more like brothers than neighbors. John thought of Jennifer then, of the two of them. No matter how close they'd been, they weren't close any more.

He wanted to change that, thought he was, until Alex came along.

"You got another letter," his mother told him as he

threaded back through the kitchen on his way upstairs. His stomach tightened. She pointed to a pink envelope sitting on the counter.

Casually, he reached for it. The handwriting was different this time.

"Who are these people writing you?" Janice went to the oven, mitts in hand.

He shrugged. "Just friends." He tucked the letter into his back pocket. Before she could ask anything more, he headed up. He'd been getting letters from girls for a while now, a strange, strange thing. Some were anonymous, filled with expressions of love, sugary poetry, even obscene things. Others were invitations to call or go on dates. He declined them, embarrassed to acknowledge the attention at all.

The phone calls were worse. How the random girls got his cell phone number, was a mystery he figured he'd never know the answer to. Most of the girls wanted to talk to him: ask if he had a girlfriend, if he wanted to hang out – what his favorite things were. Did he wear boxers or briefs? A creepy shudder ran down his back.

"You are so going to get it." His sister, Elise, came out of her bedroom and into the hall with a smile he recognized well: vengeance.

He passed her and continued to his bedroom.

"In your haste to be the next Zac Efron, you spaced taking me for my driving test today. Dad had to do it and was he pissed."

Few things got to John like being unreliable. He grew up taking on whatever came his way, first to prove to his father he could do anything, then to prove to everybody else that he could.

He'd seen the tired look on his dad's face tonight, and he'd contributed to that weariness.

"He was so mad," Elise went on, so close she almost bit his heels. "He was already mad when he came home from work, but this just pushed him over the edge. You know how bad things are right now. I can't believe you forgot."

John whirled, glaring down into her shocked eyes. The shock only lasted a second before turning into the pure pleasure of sibling power. Elise grinned. John's fingers curled and uncurled. So easily could he shove her. The temptation was more than he could resist after listening to Alex in the locker room, keeping his temper in check.

With one hand, he pushed her.

She barely rocked back on her heels, but her green eyes flamed, her long, black hair swung around her shoulders. She shoved right back.

He so wanted to shove at her again—harder this time. He was tangled up in guilt for letting his dad down.

Elise set her smug face close to his, baiting him with a sneer. Before he let himself do something he would regret later, he turned and went on to his room.

"You're a wuss," Elise called after him.

He entered the sanctuary of his bedroom and slammed the door. She'd never dare follow him in; it was a rule in their house that no one was allowed in another's space unless invited. Of course, his younger sister Katie never kept that rule. John's bedroom was the safe-haven on thunderous nights when their parents were away.

Elise ran in a few months back when the security alarm went off at two in the morning. Katie was hysterical, clinging to John and Elise as the three of them hovered in his bedroom. He thought of how he'd calmed them both, told them he was sure it was just a fluke in the system. Elise held Katie on her hip, standing in his door as he'd tip-toed off to search the house for intruders—baseball bat in hand.

The memory brought a wry smile to his face now and he crossed the room to the window.

Girls.

He looked over at Jennifer's window. No light glowed from behind the drawn shutters. It was true, whether Jenn wanted to admit it or not. Girls dug it when guys were heroes.

John stood next to Jennifer as the Vienvu family and the Michaels family formed a line around the Michaels' kitchen counter to serve themselves from the array of fragrant lasagna, crisp green salad and soft doughy breadsticks.

She said her neighborly hello when she came in, but he knew she was faking it. The hello wasn't aimed at him. She hadn't even looked at him. He figured she was still mad at him for Tingey's class.

When they were younger and fought, she'd turned her nose up at him for a few days that dragged tortuously long and dull until they made up and were friends again.

He leaned over her shoulder as she dipped the spatula into the lasagna, cutting a chunk. "Good thing we're both eating garlic tonight." He grinned when she looked at him. A spark of something disconcerting flashed on her face. He wondered why, when what the two of them did on stage was nothing compared to whatever had steamed up the windows of Alex's truck.

Jealousy stole what appetite he had, thinking of her and Alex, leaving him with lingering bitterness. He couldn't help but notice the secret smile tugging at her lips. He was pretty sure it wasn't the salad she was dishing on her plate causing it.

She was probably thinking about Alex.

In frustration he reached around her and covered her hand with his as she held the salad tongs. Their eyes met. He stole the tongs, as if the act would steal whatever was making her smile.

"Excuse me?" Jennifer's brow arched.

"Looked like you needed some help there." With a glance at his dad, John heaped a pile of greens on her plate. His cheeks flushed when his dad eyed him. "Enough?"

She looked wounded by his insinuation. "More than enough. I have six costumes to fit in."

"And you won't have a problem—eating salad."

"But I should pass on the lasagna, is that it?"

"No. Jeez." He was in trouble now.

"Six costume changes?" Janice Michaels looked at Jennifer from across the counter where she poured Kool Aid into plastic cups.

Jennifer nodded and reached for a bread stick. She held it under John's nose. "Okay with you if I eat one of these?"

John forced a smile, watching Jennifer cross the room to a spot on one of their tan leather couches. She sat and shot him a grin.

"How are rehearsals going, Jenn?" Having finished

pouring Kool Aid, Janice took her plate over. "I never get much information out of John. You know how he is."

The families gathered on the L-shaped couches, setting their plates and drinks on the dark wood coffee table nestled in the elbow of the formation.

"It's going great." Jennifer cut into her lasagna with that same grin still on her face. John thought if she was anymore pleased she'd burst. She loved it when his parents asked her questions instead of him. *She wants to play? Fine.* He sat next to her, just in case he needed to set his heel on her instep.

"John's kissing me now," Jennifer announced. The room quieted. She chewed with a smile, looking at his parents faces in the way that only she could, a way John couldn't deny was cute, like a puppy that had just gnawed a favorite slipper but you couldn't resist.

"He is, is he?" Mitchell looked at John. "You're being a gentleman?"

John appeased his dad with a nod before sending a narrow glare at Jennifer.

"Oh, he's being a gentleman." Jennifer speared a lettuce leaf with her fork. "He knows I'd bite him if he wasn't."

Everyone laughed but Jennifer's little brother, Parker, and John's little sister, Katie, who both grimaced.

"You should." The pleasure in Elise's voice was undeniable. "I'd do it. Not to John—sick. But if I had to kiss a guy and for some reason I didn't like it, I'd bite him."

"You're twisted," John told her.

"Not as twisted as you," Elise snapped back.

"Hey." Mitchell's tone warned them to put a stop to the sibling boxing match.

"I still can't believe you two are the leads." Randy took a sip of his drink. "Who'd have thought? It must be strange, you've known each other for so long."

"I imagine it makes it easier," Mitchell commented.

Far from it, John thought. Sweaty discomfort sunk to his bones. The lasagna in his stomach sat in a undigested heap. He set his fork down and let out a loud belch. The room exploded with the kind of easy laughter that comes with familiarity. He grinned, pressing his fist to his chest as another, albeit weaker burp, bubbled out.

"You know, in Tonga," Mitchell began, and everyone joined him, finishing the sentence in unison, "when you burp it's considered a compliment to the chef."

"This is excellent, Jan," Maggie said to Janice. The two mothers sat elbow to elbow on the couch. "As usual."

At that point, the mothers' heads huddled together in whispered chatter as did Randy and Mitchell. The sight gave John a sense of relief seeing his father's face lighten some, even if only temporarily.

Jennifer took another bite. John took another drink.

Gatherings like this had happened since Jennifer could remember. Why then, did she feel like she sat next to a stranger?

In her heart she missed what would have happened after dinner, had they been younger. They would have gone off into the neighborhood somewhere and created an adventure like Indian captives or mountain men.

A smile broke her lips recalling the days they'd played in "huts" they'd created from leftover construction site materials in the lower foothills just outside their back doors. Houses sat on the site now, and it was kind of sad.

"Remember when we made those huts?" She was thinking aloud more than instigating a conversation. John nodded. "Yours had to be bigger, of course," she added, looking at him.

He reached for his breadstick. "You're just jealous I finished mine first."

"Because you used the best stuff and gave me the leftovers."

John's cheeks bulged as he chewed and grinned. "Okay, okay, maybe I did that."

"No maybe about it."

After he swallowed he said, "Yeah but you were the one with the carpet."

"It was that putrid barf color." They both laughed.

"I didn't know barf putrefied."

"Well it does."

Jennifer set aside her plate because she was finished eating, and reminiscing eased the invisible strain between them. "Everybody was so jealous of our huts. They all wanted in."

Still chewing the last bit of breadstick, John nodded. "Remember our initiation ceremony? How we made everybody touch tongues, but nobody wanted to mix blood."

"Except us." Jennifer thought then how amazing it was that she carried some of him with her because of that one, childhood ritual. The thought sent a pleasant stirring around her heart.

John put his plate aside and reached for her hand, turning her palm upright. The warmth of his skin sent a tingle up her arm. With his other hand, his finger traced over the short line that some eight years earlier he had cut with his pocket knife. "You still have it."

She pulled her hand away, bringing his eyes to hers.

"Don't you?" She grabbed his hand, and he willingly opened it for her. In the exact spot where her line was, he had one just like it. Rather than touch the scar, she just looked at the light, straight line remembering that day.

He'd cut himself first, assuring her there was nothing to be afraid of. The other kids sitting around in the hot, make-shift hut were silent as the knife went in and scarlet blood oozed in droplets down John's palm. He barely made a face of pain and Jennifer knew it was because he was being watched. But she also knew if he could do it, she could do it.

Bravely she set her hand in his. He made the small incision. When her blood sprang forth, she gasped. Then he looked at her with those eyes sparkling like radiant jewels. Slowly, he took her hand and pressed their palms together.

Jennifer couldn't remember what words he'd mumbled, but she remembered a slight stinging sensation at the site. She remembered he'd looked at her during the chant.

She was still holding his hand as the memory left her, watching her thumb brush absently over his palm. His hand was completely still in hers, and she lifted her eyes to his. The corner of his jaw contracted. His gaze was tight on her face, holding her perfectly still.

"We'd probably better get going," his voice rasped a little.

Jennifer's fingers loosened around his palm and he

withdrew, rubbing his hands together. "We can't be late," she grabbed her empty plate and stood. "Chip will kill us."

John joined her. "He can't kill us, we're the stars."

"John." His mother was in the kitchen with Maggie, the two women starting to clean up. "You'll have to catch a ride to rehearsal."

"Why can't I take the car?"

"Because you won't be using it for a few days," Mitchell interjected, interrupting his conversation with Randy. The scant look of displeasure in his dad's eyes caused John's stomach to knot. He knew better than to get into a debate right then, but he hated being left at the mercy of others for transportation. His parents had no idea what that meant for him.

He looked at Jennifer, tilting her head in that know-it-all, have-it-all kind of way she did whenever he was stuck and she was the only one with a rope in sight to pull him out.

"Jenn will take you, won't you, Jenn?" Maggie pointed out.

Jennifer's lips curved into a smile that lay halfway between wicked and cute. "Sure, Maggie. I'd be more than happy to." Jennifer leaned toward him, smile mostly wicked. "But he'll have to ask me himself."

John set his teeth. "I'll call somebody else."

"You're going to inconvenience someone just so you don't have to ask me for a ride?"

"Yup." He took his plate to the kitchen and plunked it on the sink.

"No problem." She plunked hers down next to his. "Try Fletcher. He won't mind coming all the way over to give you a ride."

"Why don't you just take him?" Maggie asked.

John was in the middle of friendly fire, and he didn't want to get blasted. "Fine."

"Excuse me?" Jennifer tilted her head at him.

What was this game she played at his expense? He didn't like it, and narrowed his eyes with the promise of revenge. "You heard me."

NINE

He'd wait until just the right moment to take out that revenge. They drove to rehearsal listening to the radio because neither agreed on a CD. John thought they liked the same music, but as he browsed through her massive CD collection and noticed the punky pop CDs, it was just another reminder that things between them had changed.

He shut the black leather folder with a sigh and stared out the window. For a moment he debated dropping revenge. He needed a ride home more than he needed to salve his pride with payback.

She parked the car in the student lot. John was relieved no one else was around, though a half a dozen cars sat in the lot.

"You okay?" Jennifer asked. They strolled side-by-side. He was so quiet on the drive over, Jennifer was itchy to know why.

"Yeah, I'm fine," he said, but didn't look up from the asphalt.

"We might kill everybody with our breath. I have gum, want some?" she asked, hoping to change his mood with a change of subject.

"Yeah."

She dug in her purse. His silence bothered her enough that her own mood began to droop into darkness. Standing at the door of the building she pressed a stick of gum into his open palm. His eyes lifted to hers with something she didn't understand but caused a pinch in her heart.

The doors to the building swung open. Half a dozen cast members poured out, as if the hall was lit with dozens of fireworks—sparkling, whistling and cracking at once. Excitement and energy buzzed. The cast focused their attention on John, tugging him into the building amidst a confetti of conversation, laughter and good-natured ribbing.

Jennifer trailed behind, shaking her head. She didn't like it when the girls hooked their arms in his and hung on him. Even the boys crowded him. It reminded her of when she and John were kids and had watched black ants drag a fly underground.

"Jenn." Lacey whispered.

Jennifer stood backstage in her most uncomfortable, hottest costume, waiting for her next scene. The entire dress was velvet, like she'd rolled in the thick fabric from neck to ankles.

Lacey's costume had just a hint of velvet in the bodice. The sleeves were muslin – much cooler than hers. That annoyed Jennifer, and her tone carried it. "What?"

"You'll never guess who's out there." Lacey's grin taunted.

Jennifer fanned herself with her hands. She could care less. "Just tell me."

"Alex Jesperson. And he's brought half the team."

Jennifer's eyes opened wide. Dashing to the curtain, she peeked through. Sure enough, halfway back in the auditorium sat Alex and what looked like the first string of the Pleasant View football team. "What's he doing here?"

"I guess he came to watch." Lacey adjusted her dress, tugging the already low-cut bodice even lower.

Glancing at Lacey's bulging breasts, Jennifer said, "Lace, you're going to pop out of that."

"That's my plan. Give a little preview, snag myself a stud. You know?" When Lacey saw Jennifer roll her eyes she added, "Hey, there's plenty to go around, don't be a hog." With that Lacey made her entrance.

Jennifer looked out into the audience. She had a few minutes before she was supposed to be on stage and wondered if she should go say something to Alex. *But what?* Rachel told her that the kissing stuff was nothing more than sport.

"Your boyfriend here to watch?" There was no jesting in John's voice—coming from behind her.

Jennifer turned around.

"He's not my boyfriend." A dark storm raged in his eyes. He let out a snicker. "What?" she asked, both annoyed and curious.

"That's not what he's spreading around."

"What? What's he saying?" Grabbing his elbow, she dragged him deep into the curtains. "Tell me."

"Just that you guys were—had, you know."

"No, I do not know. Now what exactly is he saying?" The muffled voices of those playing out the scene drifted in the air. He didn't say anything, just studied her. She smelled peppermint on his breath from the gum she'd shared with him earlier.

She tugged again on his sleeve still clutched in her hand. "John, come on, tell me." Her mind raced with the nasty rumors a guy like Alex Jesperson could release with the ease of blowing his nose.

"I don't know." John looked away on a heavy sigh.

"You do and you're not telling me. Tell me."

His eyes flashed to hers. "Why? You knew what you were doing when you did whatever you did with Alex." John yanked his sleeve free. He whipped back the black curtain and disappeared into the commotion back stage.

I'm surrounded by jerks, Jennifer thought. But her discomfort was self-inflicted, a result of the night of exploration she'd spent with Alex. John was right, she had to take the consequences, whatever they were. But once rumors were out there, they were as impossible to collect as a flock of wild birds.

She made her way to Alex because she still had a few minutes before the "wedding" scene with John.

Alex sat up eagerly, his eyes sparkled, and she almost forgot why she'd ventured out into the audience. He was pretty cute. It was easy to remember how he made her feel that night, all vibrant and warm inside.

The rest of the team stared at her with fascination that comes from someone looking completely changed with the masquerade of the theater.

She crawled over bulky bodies filling the seats until she came to Alex and sat in the seat next to him.

"Hey, you look awesome," he said.

"Thanks"

"Even your costumes are classy. Cool."

"Alex, I think we need to talk. Can you stay after the rehearsal?"

"Sure."

One of the guys behind him cleared his throat. Alex glanced over. "Uh, I don't think I can stay that long. This is a long play, you know?"

"Yes, I know."

"How about we talk now?"

"I'm supposed to be on stage in five minutes."

He leaned over and surprised her with a kiss. The move stunned her. Her eyes widened, her mouth opened. "As good as I remember," he said.

Jennifer's face warmed. She bet her cheeks were pink. A quick glance around and she knew more than just the team had caught the kiss. John stood at the hem of the stage, watching. "What happened between us was just for fun, you know that right?"

Alex shrugged then nodded.

"I'd better go," she told Alex and stood.

"Yeah." Alex gave her a studly nod. She crawled back over his teammate's knees, out of the row and into the aisle.

John disappeared behind the curtain, no doubt getting in place for their scene together. Her heart beat like a wild bird was caught in her chest.

Romeo and Juliet snuck to a beautiful, secluded garden to marry. No one knew about it except Friar Lawrence. There they exchanged vows and hoped for a peaceful future.

Chip placed the three of them near the lip of the stage, in front of the artificial fountain spraying fake water. John and Jennifer were on their knees, face-to-face as Chess Wiessman, playing Friar Lawrence, stood over them, faux bible in his hands.

Chess looked down on the two of them with the approving nod of a Friar.

"A lover may bestride the gossamers that idels in the wanton summer air, and yet not fall. So light is vanity."

Jennifer replied, "Good evening to my ghostly confessor."

"Romeo shall thank thee, daughter," Chess said, "for us both."

Jennifer looked at John, extending her hands with eager joy portraying Juliet's thrill at finally being united in matrimony to her love. "As much to him, else in his thanks too much."

John took her hands. "Ah, Juliet, if measure of the joy be heaped like mine, and that thy skill be more to blazon it, then sweeten they breath this neighbors air, and let rich music's tongue unfold the imagined happiness that both receive in either by this dear encounter."

He lifted her hands. Though they'd done the move in practice, it caused her thoughts to stumble, leaving her mind blank for a second.

"Conceit," she began finally, "more rich in matter than in words, brags of his substance, not of ornament. They are but beggars that count their worth. But my true love is grown to such excess I cannot sum up sum of half my wealth."

Before she could take a breath, John let go of her hands and cupped her face. She froze. Her heart fluttered with uncertainty. At her sides, her hands hung awkward, empty, like a bird that couldn't fly. Slowly, he brought her face to his. Every sound in the auditorium melted to silence. When their lips met, Jennifer heard a soft eruption of whispers and whistles from out in the audience but she soon forgot them.

Peppermint fused with the taste of him, swirling into a heated spark that started at her mouth and sprang to her fingers and toes. Before she knew it, she leaned into him, her whole body wanting more.

When he eased back, his hands still held her face. It took her a moment to open her eyes, to breathe. She looked at his lips, wet, parted, inches from hers, then lifted her dazed eyes to his. They were sharp, almost hard with something that stole the sweetness roving in her body. She blinked once, twice, as Chess said the last line. John's hands drifted downward from her cheeks to her shoulders.

It was a look she knew well, taunting, competitive and vengeful.

She almost slapped him.

Before she could, applause and cheering tore through her thoughts, reminding her she was on stage. This was dress rehearsal; and she was acting. So was he. That infuriated her even more. He used the moment, took advantage of her to prove a point, and for what?

The lights blacked out for the scene change. Usually, John helped her to her feet so they could dart from the stage. This time he just stood, turned, and left.

Chess pulled her up. "When did we add that?" he whispered as the two of them ran offstage.

Jennifer's blood boiled, but she didn't want to look

like the idiot John was trying to make her out to be. "The other day. Chip thought it might spice things up."

Chess whistled. "Like cayenne pepper."

John stormed from the stage and out into the fluorescent–lit hall. The brief second of pleasure he'd gotten from using her vanished, now that the scene was over. He stopped at the drama room door, sent his palm flat against it in a deafening slap that burned and stung his skin. He was an idiot. She'd hate him now for sure.

The sound of feet rushing after him caused him to whirl around, ready to defend himself. But it was just some of the cast, all grins and awe.

"Dude," Drake panted, out of breath. "Was that planned or were you just, you know, caught up in the moment?"

"It was planned," John snapped, quieting the group. They kept their distance as he paced the hall.

"It was hot," Lacey grinned. "Definitely keep it in."

John stopped, scrubbed his face with his hands. "Could you guys leave me alone for a second, please?"

The little group nodded, mumbled, and begrudgingly left. He heard the door shut and assumed they'd gone, so he let his hands drop.

He didn't expect to find Jennifer there.

They stood looking at each other for a taut moment. Her hands hung in fists at her sides, her blue eyes brightened with anger. He didn't care. The vengeful act had been sweet. Seeing her in fight mode now caused any remorse he'd just felt to evaporate.

He'd talked himself out of doing anything vengeful at all, until he saw that goon Alex and his posse in the auditorium. Then something inside of him popped. It was close to popping again. "What?" he demanded.

She echoed him, "What?"

"What!"

"I can't believe you did that—in front of all those people!"

"What makes that any different than what you just did with Alex in front of all those people?"

"He kissed me, for your information!"

"I saw that!"

"Then do you need your eyes examined? *He* kissed *me*."

"I know, I know." John set anxious hands on his hips for a minute before dragging them down his face again. "Chip and I thought it would be a good place for it."

"Oh, and nobody bothered to tell me about it? I don't believe you for a second. Chip would never leave me out of it."

John lifted a shoulder. "Ask him."

"I will. You can bet I will." Jennifer whirled around and stormed back to the stage door. "And it's not staying in!"

"Yes it is!" He wasn't sure she heard him—the door slammed shut.

The cast gathered in the center of the set. Chip sat cross-legged in the middle. It was eleven o'clock and the stage stunk of sweat, resurrected costumes and paint.

Chip referred to his clipboard as he talked about the dress rehearsal, about the upcoming show, and ticket sales.

The weary cast listened, some draped over each other, others prostrate on the hard floor. Jennifer sat opposite John. She was surprised to see him sitting alone, legs crossed, elbows on his knees, fingers steepled at his mouth. His gaze locked on the stage floor.

She figured everyone was waiting for whatever chastisement he would get from Chip after the impromptu kiss, and nobody wanted to be in the line of fire when it came. He hadn't looked at her since she'd screamed at him in the hall. She still couldn't believe what he'd done. She couldn't swallow that she'd bought the moment, enjoyed it even.

Where did these random acts of weirdness come from? There was the John everybody at school worshipped. There was the John who was perfect in the eyes of adults. And the John she knew was both of those and something more, something only she was privileged to know. But that didn't ease the sting of what had happened.

He looked unusually solemn, his dark lashes nearly flat against his cheeks, his mouth set in a line. He took in a deep breath that everyone heard. Indeed, those sitting near him looked over. But his head didn't come up. He was too deep in something. *What was it?*

Her heart softened. She wanted to pinch herself, make it stop. Don't let this happen, she thought, forcing herself to look at Chip, still talking, only she had no idea about what. Chip's mouth was moving, his hands expressively painting pictures in the air. But Jennifer's mind and heart drifted back to John with such sweet ease, she found him in her sight again.

Their eyes met.

She should look away, pride demanded it. But something kept her gaze steadily with his, as if she sensed that, even with the impromptu kiss, he was silently sorry.

"And that kiss," Chip's words broke through her thoughts. He looked first at John then at her with a proud smile. "That was something else. Great job you two."

"Does it stay?" They were the first words John had uttered since the cast had been corralled for critique. He didn't look at the faces eager for his attention, he focused on Chip.

"I think it should. It's a great way to end that scene. Agreed?"

John nodded and lowered his head again.

"Jenn?" Chip looked at her.

They were right. It meant she'd kiss John not once, but twice during the performances. A familiar skittering of pleasure ran along her spine. "Okay."

TEN

The drama room reeked. There was no other word for the mixture of body odor, soiled costumes and stale breath. As actors changed out of their costumes Taunia ran from cast member to wardrobe rack and the scent in the room ripened, bodies now exposed in the cloistered air.

"Somebody open a freakin' window," Drake called.

Nobody wanted to look like a prude, hovering in a corner while they changed, so modesty was ditched at the door.

Pleasant View High School was characteristically outdated. That meant no male and no female dressing rooms. That meant communal dressing.

John changed, keeping his eyes on his pile of discarded costumes. One stray glance could start a conversation. Worse, somebody would ask him for a ride home and everybody would find out that he didn't have a car.

Then his life would become a circus.

Everybody was tired so nobody did much talking. He was glad for that. But he had to keep an eye on Jennifer to make sure she didn't leave without him. He chanced looking across the room at her.

She always dressed and undressed with her back to everyone. He liked that about her. Lacey and the other girls practically changed costumes right under his nose. His mind flashed a picture of Jennifer that night he'd opened the drama room door and found her in her underwear. A hot flush filled him from head to toe as he pulled his shirt over head. He'd never forget the sight.

"Dude, can I catch a ride?" Fletcher zipped up his jeans as he strolled over.

"Can't tonight. Sorry."

Though everybody tried not to look over, John knew by the way the room went silent his refusal was overheard. Now everybody wondered why.

Startled by the rejection, Fletcher said, "Oh."

John sat in the desk where he'd piled his discarded costumes and pulled on his pants. "I don't have a car," he said quietly.

"I can give you a ride," Lacey piped.

Drake moved closer as well. "I'm going right by your house, dude."

"I can give you a lift." Andrew pulled a sweatshirt over his head. "I have the suburban."

John looked up into the faces of half of the cast surrounding him. Pressure inside began to build. Sweat sprung at his armpits, behind his neck. He looked over at Jennifer. She was finished dressing and now gathered her backpack and purse.

It was naive of him to think she'd forget about the unscripted kiss and give him a ride, but he was too tired to take a ride with someone wanting something from him, even a conversation. Jennifer would give him the silent treatment. That much he deserved.

"I already have a ride," he said, waiting for her reaction. Her fast exit from the drama room had him bolting up, snatching his stuff, and following her.

He let her keep a good ten foot lead in the hall as they headed to the parking lot. He closed the distance between them as soon as their feet hit pavement. Sure, he could get a ride with somebody if she full-on left him, but he really was sorry for using the moment onstage like he had.

"Jenn." He didn't expect her to stop. She'd make any communication difficult. She had her back to him as they half-jogged to her yellow VW. "I'm sorry about what I did," he blurted.

She stopped and faced him, nearly causing him to bump right into her. They stood in the quiet of night, the distant sound of an occasional car humming down the street mixing with the singing of crickets. "Say it again—to my face."

"I'm sorry about that."

"You're not sorry." She walked the last stretch to her car and stuck her keys in the lock then opened the door. "I know you, and I know when you're sorry. And that was not sorry."

"I am too." He pushed her door shut and held it closed with his hand. "You don't know anything."

"I know that you can't say you're sorry and look me in the eye."

"I just did."

"You said 'I'm sorry about that' and you were looking at...at everything but me."

"Was not. So?"

"So it wasn't a true apology."

His eyes flicked over her face, his teeth set. "So, what, you're not going to give me a ride because of it?"

Jennifer tilted her head. She liked that he squirmed just a little, he deserved it. But she couldn't hold onto the anger long. So what if he hadn't looked her right in the eye, he looked so... something melancholy hovered in his expression, as if he wasn't sure he could trust her and was sad because of it.

"I have to go," she said, pulling on the door he still held pinned. His other hand slapped the roof of the car, jolting her. "Calm down, John."

Thrusting both hands through his hair he turned away, facing the school. The muscles in his shoulders and back tensed. "Okay, fine," she said. "Come on." She got in the car and started the ignition. "But you owe me."

He looked at her with disbelief, as if she'd betrayed him with the statement and it took her back for a moment. "Just kidding," she offered.

A lamp burned in his father's office window. His father was working at home. The house was quiet, yet John didn't even consider going to bed without first doing what he had to do.

He knocked at the open door of his dad's office.

His father looked up from his work. He set down his pen and ran his hands down his face. Then he leaned back in the leather swivel chair and looked at John. After a thoughtful pause he waved him in.

John's stomach churned. He walked to the desk, hands wringing. Golden lamplight cast a soft glow through the dark room and across his father's tired face.

"Late night?" John asked even though the answer

was obvious.

"Yeah. How was rehearsal?"

John shrugged. "Late. Long."

"You ready? Isn't opening night coming up?"

John nodded.

His father leaned forward on his elbows, waiting.

John thought of Jennifer, of her accusation that he couldn't apologize and wished she could see him now. "Sorry about today."

"Okay. What happened?"

"Mr. Daniels asked me to help him with something. I lost track of the time."

His father nodded and rested his chin on his hands. He let out a sigh. "You lost the privilege of using the car because we both know this isn't the first time you've stretched yourself too thin. You've got too much on your plate when you start forgetting things."

John nodded.

"Is there anything that can give?"

John lifted his shoulders. "Student council goes till the end of the year. The play runs two weeks. Track starts in four. Chamber choir goes for the rest of the year and I have peer tutoring that needs me until finals. I start that job at the retirement center in a month."

"You can't cut the play. There would be no Romeo and Juliet without Romeo. But something else has to go. You can do better than this."

"But the play will be over and—"

"Trim the fat, whatever is absolutely unnecessary." He picked up his pen and lowered his head, a signal that he was finished counseling.

John went to his bedroom with his heart heavier

knowing what his father expected. And he was right. But his schedule wasn't unlike many of his friends and they all seemed to handle theirs without things leaking at the seams.

He sat on his bed with a groan. He was bound to student council; there was no way out of that. He was part of the blood that kept the school running.

His track coach, Mr. Ivers, had made it perfectly clear that he was expected to perform to perfection so they could get another state championship under their belts. Dropping track was out of the question.

He'd never give up the play; it was the one thing he was really enjoying, even with the added strain of learning seven-hundred and thirty-four lines.

Chamber choir had a tour coming up, which meant he'd be gone singing with the group for days at a time.

He rubbed his face. A dozen students depended on his help during peer tutoring hour. Even though that was voluntary, it was another thing he couldn't drop. He thought of Runt, of how far he'd come since they'd worked on algebra together. No one knew that John had been trying to help the painfully shy kid come out of his skin a little as they reviewed algebra. It had taken months to get the guy to even say hi to a girl.

He needed money, so bagging a job op wasn't an option.

For a while he lay under the heaviness of a suffocating decision. A couple of years ago nobody cared or noticed if he dropped an elective or gave up a volunteer job. Those days were gone, and the memory of anonymity caused his stomach to crimp.

The past few years were a blur. The constant

attention from students he'd never seen before and teachers who suddenly knew his name overwhelming. At first the notoriety was flattering, but he realized very quickly that being watched meant acting responsibly.

He rolled onto his side and looked out the window. Jennifer's bedroom light was on, but the shutters were drawn.

He longed for a crude tin can and some string.

She was mad at him and would scream in his ear through that makeshift can before she would ever give him any advice. *What did she know, anyway?* No one really understood what it was like to be under a magnifying glass unless they were a captured insect.

John pushed himself up off the bed, even though he was weary to the bone. One last thing to do so he could sleep with a clear conscience. Unlocking his window, he opened it wide and looked across at the soft glow coming from Jennifer's bedroom. Then he scanned his floor, but it was freshly vacuumed and there were no scraps, nothing he could use.

A colorful ceramic tray from Mexico sat on the table next to his bed. It held leftover change whenever he had any. He grabbed a penny, aimed and threw. The penny hit the glass with a clink then fell silently to the grass below. When nothing happened, he grabbed another and threw again. This time the blinds flew up and Jennifer peeked out, looking at first startled, then annoyed when she saw him. But she opened her window.

"What?"

John pressed his hands into the window casing. She wore something pink and grey: a nightshirt that buttoned up the front. But the top button was undone. Her hair was in a pony tail, spilling over the top of her head as she leaned out the window. Her face was ivory-pink, like she'd just taken a bath.

"I'm sorry," he said.

He liked that he surprised her. She didn't even blink. When she nodded, the curl at the end of her pony tail bounced and teased.

" 'Night," he said.

" 'Night, John."

When she said his name, something warm slid through him, settling his tight nerves. His dad told him it was good business to use the name of everyone you talk to. John just though it was cool, so he'd started doing that a few years ago. But nothing was cooler than having Jennifer call him by name. Right now, that was the best thing.

ELEVEN

"People," Chip began. The cast of Romeo and Juliet was scattered through the drama room, listening as they readied for their first performance, a matinee Pleasant View hosted for neighboring elementary schools. The performance enabled the actors to iron out any wrinkles before an uncritical, mostly inattentive audience. The cast and crew didn't mind since they got out of classes for the day.

"This is what I call our wet run—wet behind the ears if you will. By tonight, we'll be dry as a baby's butt."

"Like you'd know," Andrew chided. "You don't have any kids."

Chip smiled, nodded. "But I am an uncle. Now." His smile dropped into a serious line across his face. "If there is any, and I repeat *anything* that comes up during performance, and I guarantee there will be, the show goes on. I told you the story of when I was in Robin Hood and twisted my ankle. No one knew it until after the show. Then I screamed. Then I swore. Then I was rushed to the ER." Chip looked into every face soberly. He settled on John and Jennifer. "You two especially—improvise. That's what this performance is for, to see if we have any bugs to work out. Got it?"

Chip waved everyone together for a familial hug. They linked arms in a large circle and bowed their heads.

He gave a short, inspirational speech.

"Everybody hits makeup and hair," Chip ordered after, pointing to the lit glass vanity where pots of makeup were scattered. Brushes for both hair and face shot up like mink blossoms from miniature vases. The boys groaned. The girls willingly sought the palettes and hair instruments, eager to transform themselves.

"Jenn." Chip went to her. "You're the best with this stuff. I want everyone to pass your inspection before going onstage. Everybody hear that?"

Most of the boys grinned and smiled at her. Everybody crowded around the small, mirrored vanity and, with a little nudging, reached for this and that.

"Do I have enough red stuff on my cheeks?" Freshly powdered, Drake stepped back for all to see.

"You look demented, dude."

"Like Bozo, man."

"Perv."

"Here." Jennifer went to him with a soft sponge and blotted his cheeks. Drake stood perfectly still, eyes locked on her every move.

"Hey," Andrew whined. "I got too much blush on too, Jenn." He stuck his face next to hers, his eyes closed and his lips pursed.

"Everybody needs some blush on their cheeks," Jennifer explained, laughing at the joke. "Or you'll look dead on stage. The lights wash you out."

"And eyeliner." Lacey taunted, waving a liner wand with relish. The boys groaned. She went to John.

He stepped back. "No way."

"Even you need it, John." Lacey brought the wand to his eyes but he held up both hands in protest.

"No, he doesn't." Trish looked over from the makeup table "He's got dark eyelashes already."

"Let's ask Jenn," Lacey said. "Jenn, does John have to wear eyeliner or not?"

Jennifer looked over from her blotting job on Drake's cheeks. There was no denying John had thick, black lashes—they could be seen from across the football field, let alone the room.

"He wears it," Jennifer said firmly, taking a moment to enjoy the way John's eyes widened.

"I protest," John said. The room erupted in laughter. Lacey set her fingers on his chest and playfully pushed him into a nearby chair.

Jennifer's stomach knotted with jealousy.

"It's easy, dude." Fletcher had his own tube and, nose pressed to the mirror, painted on a coat of the black stuff. "Even I can—ouch!" He blinked and the wand smeared into his eye. "This stuff stings!"

Laughing, Jennifer dampened a paper towel and rushed over, wiping just underneath his eye. "Boys are such babies. Stand still or it'll get all over everything," she told him.

"Hey," Fletcher piped. "Can you kiss it and make it all better?"

Lifting to her toes, Jennifer placed a kiss just under his eye.

"I stabbed myself with the lip liner." Drake held up a burgundy pencil, pointing to his lower lip. "Right here."

"Yeah, right." Jennifer went back to looking at Fletcher's eye. "Only one more coat, okay? And be careful."

"This thing's just as dangerous as a rapier." Fletcher

returned to the mirror to apply more of the black muck.

Jennifer was glad everyone went back to readying themselves. Only John was looking at her under narrowed eyes, a deep crease between his dark brows.

How could something meant to be a gesture of good will curl his insides like he'd just witnessed murder? John sat in the chair like a prisoner, unable to get up and keep her from spreading her kisses to every guy in the room.

"Save it for the stage," he snapped.

Jennifer finished blotting Drake's cheek and looked over her shoulder. A tense hush blanketed the room and she turned, setting one hand on her hip. "I have plenty to go around."

"That's what I hear." John shot up out of the chair, moving Lacey aside.

Jennifer's other hand fisted on her hip. "You keep saying that, only you don't have the guts to tell me what it is, or the nerve to check out what you hear before believing it."

"I don't need to check it out." John met her halfway in the middle of the room. "I can see it."

"And what do you see?"

"You're kissing every guy you can get your hands on."

Jennifer didn't dare glance around into the silenced faces of everyone watching. Her eyes flushed with tears, and soon those tears would stream down her face. "Why do you care?"

"I have to kiss you, don't I? I don't want leftovers."

Hushed whistles and murmurs of disbelief pierced the air. No one moved, standing as shameless observers.

One tear did escape then, and it ran down the side of Jennifer's face. He thought she was used goods—that hurt. Her lower lip gave way, trembling. In all of her years learning the craft of acting, she'd never been able to control her lower lip when her emotions broke loose. But she had learned she could exit gracefully. So she did.

She found a deserted corner in a forgotten hall. She wasn't alone for long. Bodies gathered behind her. She heard whispering and somebody placed a hand on her shoulder.

"Jenn?" Taunia asked.

"Is she okay?" She recognized Fletcher's voice; it was his hand on her shoulder.

"What a jerk," Trish said.

"Yeah," somebody agreed.

Jennifer made herself think of the play, of performing, of losing herself in the show. *That's the beauty of acting.* She thrust up her chin and sniffed. She wiped at her cheeks before facing those who had come out to check up on her.

"It's nothing," she said. "He's a jerk, that's all."

The heads surrounding her nodded in sober agreement but Jennifer knew most of them probably thought John's indiscretion was warranted somehow.

They followed her back into the drama room, quieter now as she entered. She was keenly aware that everyone, including John, who was slipping on his white, blousy shirt, watched her. She refused to look at him but she smiled at everyone else, sorry her eyes were red, making her look like she cared about what had happened. And she did, no matter how she tried to convince herself that she didn't.

She finished dressing with her back to the room, not speaking to anyone.

Ty, the stage manager, called everyone to the curtain and the cast gathered there in a somber mood, waiting for the music to cue up, for Chip to greet and welcome the young students in the audience.

And then it was time.

How will I ever touch him, kiss him, feeling the way I do? Wouldn't that be something, to push him away right in front of everyone? But that would not be true to Juliet.

Jennifer's cell phone vibrated on the bed next to her. She picked it up. Rachel. It was impossible to think that out of a cast and crew of fifty, no one would say anything about the incident. ennifer didn't mind the limelight; she just didn't like it spilling offstage into her personal life.

"I heard what happened," Rachel said. "I can't believe he called you a ho."

"He didn't call me that."

"I heard you called him your pimp, you know, with all the action you guys are getting together onstage."

It seemed like a very bad dream with no end, this round of rumors. "Neither one of us said anything like that."

Rachel sighed. "Oh. Well, then what *did* happen?"

"He told me he didn't like me kissing every boy I got my hands on because he has to kiss me, and he doesn't like kissing used goods."

"He said, 'used goods'?"

"His exact words were, 'I don't want leftovers'."

"What a jerk," Rachel hissed. "He's more than a jerk. He's a—"

"Rache, it's okay." But the words echoed in her hollow heart and the sting of tears bloomed behind her eyes again. The more she thought about it, the more incensed she became.

Rachel wouldn't get it. Rachel handled boys with the ease of picking the ripest fruit at the grocery store, taking a bite or two and tossing it when she'd had enough. For Jennifer, males were much more complicated because the largest part of her heart was still occupied with thoughts of only one.

Jennifer rolled onto her stomach. "I'm wasted. I need to get some sleep," she said. "Tomorrow's opening night and if I don't feel better, I'm going to stab myself with the knife for real."

"He's playing games with you. I can see a player a mile away."

"Why would he do that?"

"He probably likes you."

Something pleasant swarmed in Jennifer's stomach. "You're way wrong."

"How long have you two been playing at this love to hate each other thing?"

"We're not playing at anything."

"You two practically invented it. I mean, how many people have known each other as long as you two? Living within twenty feet—he's practically part of the family."

"And we're more like brother and sister than— than—" Jennifer couldn't bring herself to verbalize the words boyfriend and girlfriend.

"He's not leaving it alone, Jenn," Rachel went on.
"That means he cares. He may not know that he cares.
He may not admit it. But I bet that's why he's acting
bipolar."

"You think?" Jennifer went to her window and
looked across into John's. "But he's being so mean."

"It's totally playground, I know." Rachel had worldly
wisdom that had earned Jennifer's admiration. "But some
guys are stuck there. Yes, even guys like John Michaels.
Think about it. Who was he three years ago? A nobody
with a nice tan."

"Yeah, I know."

"And suddenly he's Mr. Hottie that every girl wants.
Go figure."

"Why?" They'd had this discussion before, but
neither girl tired of dissecting the social status quo at
Pleasant View High School.

"Have you looked back at our yearbooks from
junior high? The guy wore his hair like he'd just come from
boot camp. And he had braces."

Jennifer smiled. John's mother had complained
about John's fifteen cowlicks since Jennifer could
remember. John wore the short cut out of necessity. But
he'd grown it longer in high school, and that, coupled
with the normal changes of muscling out and growing
up, had created someone totally hot.

"Your problem is you happen to have taste like
ninety-nine percent of females," Rachel said.

"And you don't think John's hot?"

"From a strictly physical standpoint, yeah, he
pretty much defines stud. But he's got major issues with

perfectionism."

"You know, I always thought that too." Jennifer leaned against the window, still staring across into John's. "He's been like that forever."

"*Of course.*" Rachel reminded her of their coined phrase—of course— they attached to anything and all things John. "Nobody tries that hard to please at our age. We're too self-absorbed."

Not him, Jennifer thought with such sappy ease she wanted to kick herself. *Just hours ago he humiliated me in front of the cast. I should be livid.* But she knew who John was beneath the captivating eyes and brilliant smile. It was in memories of the way he helped her mother unload groceries; of how he mowed their lawn when her dad was gone on a business trip; or defended her little brother from a neighborhood brat that brought Jennifer's heart back to him, even after arguments, after years of distance. Even after what happened today.

She said goodbye to Rachel and hung up the phone staring out into the darkness of his room. It wasn't fair. He really was the nicest guy she knew. She couldn't help that she liked him.

She thought about what had happened at the matinee, how he'd acted – dare she think the word— jealous. Rachel's suggestion that he was playing some kind of game, that he really did like her, sounded as foreign in her ears as the Chinese language.

She decided not to entertain the possibility, knowing how easily she could be lost to it, hopelessly lost, only to be heartbroken when nothing happened.

Friends are always just friends. And that's all she and John would ever be.

TWELVE

Only one line forgotten so far, pretty good for an opening night. Jennifer remembered last year's play, *Some Like It Hot.* Dirk Jasper had completely missed an entrance. They'd found him in the boys bathroom, puking.

Jennifer doubted John had eaten dinner. She looked across the stage at him as she crouched in the tomb where Romeo was to discover Juliet "dead." He watched the other players, drawn in or concentrating on his entrance, she wasn't sure. His hands opened and closed. The bones in his jaw flexed every now and then— he looked totally hot.

Feeling warm, she fanned her face with her hands. *Oh, well, I could blame it on the lights,* she thought. It didn't help that his costume accentuated his lean frame. He wore beige tights underneath a long, paisley tunic. He had a reckless, pirate look about him. He'd unbuttoned the top button of his shirt, revealing the dark skin at the hollow of his throat. His long sleeves were rolled up. He'd hear from Chip after the show. Chip had warned that no one was to alter their costumes in any way during performance—even under the sweat of hot lights.

Their death scene was coming. Romeo would come across her lying there, and thinking her dead, drink of the vial and kill himself. Juliet would awaken and stab herself, covering him with her body.

The scene was the climax of the show and in rehearsal John did it well. She thought he could give more of himself to it, but knew how hard it was to let go in front of an audience.

He made his entrance and began one of his final monologues as he fought with Paris.

"Wilt thou provoke me? Then have at thee, boy!"

She heard the rapiers clang as steel sliced steel. Heard the boys grunt, the heavy thudding of feet. Then, one big thud as Paris fell.

"Oh, I am slain! If thou be merciful, open the tomb. Lay me with Juliet."

Jennifer readied for the cardboard "rock" to be rolled back, revealing her. John always stumbled on this next monologue and butterflies filled her stomach for him. His voice drifted up underneath the cardboard set.

"Said he not so? Or did I dream it so? Or am I mad, hearing him talk of Juliet?"

Without any mistakes, John recited the half-page monologue and then opened the tomb. She closed her eyes and focused on lying still. She felt him rush toward her, then kneel at her side.

As practiced, he grabbed her hands, bringing them to his chest.

"Oh, my love, my wife!" He kissed her hands. *"Death, that hath sucked the honey of thy breath, hath no power yet upon thy beauty."* His voice choked with more emotion than Jennifer had ever heard and she almost peeked through her lashes at him.

Brilliant waves of electricity danced in the air around them. Excitement sprang through her senses.

"Thou art not conquered yet. In crimson thy lips and in thy cheeks, and death's pale flag is not advanced there—"

All of a sudden, his arms scooped under her back and he lifted her against him. He continued the speech. Jennifer forced herself to remain docile, even though the spontaneous move shot rocketing tremors through her system.

One of his hands stroked her face as he spoke. *"From this world-wearied flesh. Eyes, look your last. Arms, take your last embrace. And lips, O you the doors of breath, seal with a righteous kiss a dateless bargain to engrossing death."*

She didn't dare open her eyes, but her body tensed. He held her cradled tight, one hand cupping her face. His breath brushed her lips and her heart sped in her chest. In practice he had only held her hands and wept over her, and then drunk from the vial before falling dead. His fingers were light at her mouth now, tracing her lips as he sobbed; then in a shocking move, the heat of his mouth was on hers.

She tasted salty tears. The warm urgency of his lips sent a ravaging shiver through every part of her and as he slowly drew back, she fought her natural response to open her eyes and look at him.

"Come bitter conduct, come unsavoury guide."

Still holding her against him, he reached for the poisonous vial, finishing the monologue with wrenching emotion. *"Thy drugs are quick! Thus with a kiss, I die."*

He crumpled over her in a different position than he had during their weeks of rehearsal. His impromptu actions now left them entwined like a pretzel. For a moment she could hardly breathe under his weight.

They lay in a moment of complete silence. She had the sudden urge to fold her arms around him. There was no response from the audience. It was as if they weren't there.

Friar Lawrence entered and gave his startled lines to the Chief Watchman and the Page who came bearing flowers to the tomb. Jennifer began to awaken as Juliet. She eased out from under John as smoothly as she could, gently rolling him to the side.

"O comfortable Friar! Where is my lord? I do remember well where I should be, and there I am. Where is my Romeo?"

Because John had changed the scene and Romeo was so obviously on top of her, Jennifer improvised, immediately discovering him. She looked at him, saw the tears staining his face and almost forgot her line.

"What's here? A cup, closed in my true love's hand? Poison, I see, hath been his timeless end. O churl, drunk all and left no friendly drop to help me after? I will kiss thy lips. Haply some poison yet doth hang on them, to make me die with a restorative." She was supposed to lean over and make it look like she was giving him one last kiss. But the way John had rolled Jennifer knew a faux kiss would never cut it.

She leaned over, turned his face up and lowered her lips to his. Maybe it was because he couldn't respond, that his lips were utterly still beneath hers, but a buzz of lightening jagged from her mouth and settled low inside of her. The scent of his sweat and shampoo drifted in her head. His breath held a moment, then trickled, teasing every nerve on her face.

Slowly, Jennifer sat up and took the dagger in her hand, looking at it. *"Then I'll be brief. O happy dagger, this is thy sheath. There rust and let me die."* She made herself fall over him and held her breath.

The remaining cast slowly took their places around them on stage. She tried to slow her breathing as Chip had instructed so she appeared dead, but with each breath, the pain in her lungs sharpened.

She barely thought of what the other characters were reciting, she could only concentrate on holding still—on not breathing. Her heart pounded. It seemed every ounce of blood rushed to her head and pooled there.

The final scene seemed to take forever, and as the last words were spoken, Jennifer saw sparkles behind her closed eyes, deeper black and then nothing.

"For never was a story of more woe that this of Juliet and her Romeo."

The lights blacked out and the room shook with applause. It was nearly pitch black back stage, but everyone knew where they were supposed to go for curtain call.

John reached out to Jennifer. "Jenn?"

When she didn't respond, he gently shook her. "Jenn?" Panic filled him. "Jenn, it's time. We have to move." When she didn't respond, he scooped her up and headed behind the black stage curtains and knelt down. Everyone quickly gathered around.

"What happened?"

"Is she okay?"

"Should we get Chip?"

John leaned close, wondering if she was just playing

a trick. "This is no time to be getting back at me, Vienvu," he whispered. She didn't move. Sweat drenched his face and he swiped his sleeve across his brow.

"Curtain call!" Ty whispered.

Jennifer stirred, a little moan squeaking from her throat. Then her eyes opened. She stared into hovering faces.

"Jenn?" A sigh escaped John's chest. "You okay?"

"What happened?"

"You blacked out."

"Curtain!" Ty called, this time louder.

The cast scattered to their positions. Jennifer tried to sit up but blinked hard and wobbled back.

John pulled her up and held her steady. "Maybe you'd better—"

"No." She shook her head. "I can do it. I have to do it. Chip will kill me."

"What if you faint again?" He had her arm and she glanced at where his fingers met her skin. "I'll help you."

"No, really, I can do it." With a determined tug she was free, and started to her curtain call position on the opposite side of the stage. John barely heard the cheers and applause when the curtain slid open. His nerves still rattled from Jennifer's brush with unconsciousness.

The cast took their bows in order of importance. Applause intensified when she and John walked toward each other, joined hands, then continued to the front of the stage for their bow.

It was hot under the lights. Jennifer felt a slight buckling in her knees warning her that she might faint again. She bowed first with John, then as he stood back applauding her, she bowed alone. A strange excitement filled her. They took one last bow to the now-standing audience. It was the first time she'd suffered for her art. The feeling was oddly electrifying.

There was so much energy on stage; she ignored the dizziness in her head. The curtain fell and the cast erupted into laughter and congratulatory hugs. The woozy feeling deepened with every squeeze and hug until finally, her heart started racing. Those familiar sparkles twirling in darkness danced behind her eyes again.

"Jenn, something's wrong." Why John was next to her suddenly, she didn't know but she was glad all the same.

"It's nothing." There were so many people clamoring around them, talking all at once. She tried to steady her breath. "Maybe I should sit down."

She couldn't help that she enjoyed the way John's arm protectively cupped around her, or the way he took charge, pushing through everyone to find a place for her.

"Jenn needs to rest," he boomed.

"Is she okay?"

"What happened?"

"I'll bet she stabbed herself."

"I think she fainted."

"I'd faint too if John kissed me."

"I'd full-on freak if John kissed me."

"Guys, leave her alone." John found an empty chair, set both of his hands on her shoulders and eased her carefully into it, staying close, as if ready to draw his rapier in case anybody hovered over her.

Chip finally made his way backstage. He grinned with pride from ear to ear. "Guys, gather round. That was awesome, just awesome. John, you were insane. Insane! I loved it!"

When he found his cast quiet and inquisitive, his grin dropped. "Something happen?"

"Dude, it's Jenn." Drake tilted his head Jennifer's direction. Chip quickly broke through the cast to go to her. "What happened?"

"She fainted," John said.

"I'm sure it's nothing." Jennifer wondered about her performance. Chip hadn't said anything about it.

"Let's get you somewhere you can lie down." Chip looked around.

"My mom's here," Lacey announced. "She's an RN. Want me to find her?"

Chip nodded, but didn't look relieved. With a jerk of his head, he gestured for John to follow him. "Let's take her to the drama room."

He faced the group. "I want everybody to go out front and greet the audience."

Loyalty to Chip kept everyone from mumbling as they changed course toward the stage door.

"Jeez, Jenn," Chip eyed her as he and John walked with her to the drama room. "Did you skip dinner?"

"No." Her face heated.

"You should have skipped curtain call."

"And ruin the perfect performance?" She tried to hide the sarcasm but a thread still remained. "The show must go on, right?"

She looked up at John. His brows were knit tight, his eyes somewhere between angry and worried. "You did great out there."

His face softened. He pushed open the door of the

drama room and held it for her.

"You feeling okay?" Chip asked her again.

"Yes. Yes."

John's voice was hard. "It was my fault."

"Jenn, sit down." Understandable concern laced Chip's voice as he led her to an empty chair and made her sit.

"I threw her off." John's hands squeezed nervously. "I fell across her the wrong way. I put too much pressure on her, lying across her like that. She couldn't breathe—"

Chip set a hand on John's shoulder. "Stop. It's not your fault. Great improvised kiss, by the way. It stays."

Jennifer's eyes met John's. Her insides fluttered.

The door flew open and Lacey hurried in with her mother behind. "Here she is."

"Hey everybody." Ann Naeverson wore tight jeans and an even tighter sweater over a cello shaped figure. She looked like Lacey's older sister rather than her mother, her dark hair stylishly flipped out, her wrists and fingers glittering with jewelry. She had Lacey's flirty smile under brilliant green eyes.

"Thanks for coming." Chip moved aside so she could get to Jennifer.

"I'm Ann. You faint honey?" Ann leaned toward Jennifer for a look. Then she dug into her bright flowered purse and pulled out what looked like a nail kit in brilliant pink. "Maybe you fellas better wait outside."

Chip nodded and he and John left the room.

The crowd was thick and still enthusiastic and when John and Chip emerged from the hall it erupted into another round of applause.

Chip was swallowed up by the cast while John

suddenly found himself surrounded by faces, some he knew, most he didn't. He hated having to smile—to act. His mind was on Jennifer and what happened. Voices rushed in and out of his head. He couldn't look at any one person. Too many faces, too close. Everybody talked at once and people were touching him.

"You were so good."

"Were those real swords?"

"Are you wearing tights?"

"He looks hot in them."

"I know."

"Is it fun? Being in the play?"

"So are you, like, going to be an actor or something?"

"I think he'd be good."

"Better than Brad Pitt."

"Hotter than Orlando Bloom."

"Totally."

John dragged his hands down his face, and looked over his shoulder, back toward the doors of the drama room.

Mr. Daniels approached with a grin. "John, you did a great job." Extending his right hand, his left encircled his wife standing next to him with their children nestled close to her. She nodded in glowing agreement.

"Thank you."

"I didn't know you were an actor."

"Yeah, well, I'm not sure one play qualifies me."

"Pretty convincing. Shakespeare's not easy."

His wife nodded with awe-struck enthusiasm. "Brought tears to my eyes, that death scene."

"Oh yeah?" John's face warmed from the

compliment.

"Yeah, you were totally awesome," a girl standing to his left added. "I mean, the way you cried at the end was so hot."

John rubbed the back of his neck and forced a smile. He couldn't enjoy the compliments, not while Jennifer was back there. He wanted to find out what was wrong. A feathering of panic caused him to excuse himself and sneak to the drama room.

Three girls trailed behind him. "John, where are you going?" one asked, waving her program.

He barely slowed as he turned around. "Uh, to the drama room for a minute."

"But you're coming back out here, right?"

"Maybe."

He knocked, but when he didn't hear anything he opened the door, afraid something had gone wrong. Jennifer had changed into a pink warm-up sweat suit. Lacey and her mom sat perched on desks. They looked like a group of girls just hanging together, talking and laughing.

John stepped through the door. The heavy metal shut with a clank that had all of their heads turning his direction.

"Hey." Lacey hopped off the desk, approaching him with her hips in a languid swing.

John's eyes fixed on Jennifer. "You okay?" He was glad she smiled. Something deep inside of him sighed.

"Just like I thought," she told him. "Lacey's mom figures I was air deprived."

He strode over. "So she's going to be okay?"

"Probably a mix of nerves and your hotness." Lacey

tapped his shoulder. "Any girl would faint after a kiss like that."

John dipped his head. Then he looked at Jennifer. "That's a first for you, isn't it?" he asked.

"I've never fainted before, if that's what you mean."

"You two must know each other pretty well if you know she's never fainted before." Ann Naeverson arched a brow.

"They're like next door neighbors." Lacey moved closer to John but he barely noticed, his eyes still fixed on Jennifer.

"I told her to take slow, shallow breaths during that last scene," Ann said. "But there's nothing I can do about the wow behind that kiss."

John averted a face of embarrassment. "Yeah, well, she's used to it."

"Used to it?" Ann cackled. "A girl never gets used to it, honey. Trust me." She patted his shoulder, picked up her purse and slung it over her arm. "Maybe you'd better move on, if she's used to it. Spread some of that sizzle around, if you know what I mean. Lacey here wouldn't mind, would you honey?"

Lacey gleamed. "John, you were so awesome tonight. I didn't get a chance to tell you before, with, you know, what happened."

"If you don't need me anymore, I'll wait outside." Ann tapped over to the door in her red stilettos. "I'm going to talk to Mr. Chips about being on hand for medical emergencies." She waved a hand, her bracelets jangled, her rings glittered, and she was out the door.

"She's hot for Chip," Lacey muttered. "It sucks

having a single mom. Anyway." She stood directly in John's path, blocking him from any exit. "You were so great, John. Seriously."

Jennifer rolled her eyes and stooped to pick up one of her costumes that had fallen to the floor when she'd changed. She'd never hear the end of John's award-winning performance, she was sure of that. And she'd missed her opportunity to stand out front and hear her own accolades.

Feeling dizzy on the way up, Jennifer made a little sound, bringing John to her side. "You should take it slow," he said.

"I'm taking it slow," Jennifer snapped, holding the slip in front of his face.

"I could have gotten it."

"Look." Jennifer tilted her head. "I fainted. I'm not made of glass."

"Plastic maybe?"

Jennifer wanted to slug him, but with Lacey looking on she had to protect her reputation. She settled for glaring.

Behind them, Lacey swung her hips. "John?"

He didn't look at Lacey because he was glaring into her eyes. "What?"

"Since my mom's going to be schmoozing Chip for a while, I was wondering if you could give me a ride home?"

Her voice was sweeter than corn syrup. Jennifer sneered out a laugh. She gathered the rest of her things.

"I don't have a car," John told her.

"He's grounded from it," Jennifer informed Lacey, without sparing John a glance. She could tell he was seething by the way his body drew tight next to her. Smiling, she headed for the door. "As his next door neighbor I know these things."

THIRTEEN

There weren't any lingering affects from the fainting. Most of Jennifer's suffering was due to the fact that the air at Pleasant View High School thickened with praise for John's performance, Chip's directorial efforts, and the quality of the production in general.

Oh, her fainting incident was up there on the hot-whisper-of-the-day list, but she took very little enjoyment for the notoriety. She wanted to hear how great she'd done as Juliet, not, "Did you really faint from John's kiss?"

Jennifer's blood boiled.

She tucked the school newspaper under her arm and made her way to class. It didn't matter that people she'd never met smiled at her with awe. She'd taken drama in school since junior high, and she'd auditioned for and made every play in the interim. She'd secured the coveted crown of Chip's favorite. She was set to ride on a full drama scholarship in the college of her choice, if she didn't choose English as a major instead.

Then John came along.

John who, from the inception of their lives as neighbors, had been racing her up the ladder to the top, and now stole the one crown she wore right off of her head.

For years she thought she was just imagining the competitive wall they were climbing. Her mother told her she overreacted, part of the drama queen thing. Now, Jennifer knew that the wall was real.

"Great job last night." Somebody tapped her shoulder in the mass of bodies in the hall. She turned around but didn't know who the smiling blonde boy was.

"Thanks."

She should enjoy this, but all she felt was the familiar simmering of ever-present jealousy whenever she and John were involved in anything together. She felt like the Grinch.

As she neared English she saw his dark hair like a black buoy bobbing in a sea of admirers. She heard his name, the high-pitch of girls' laughter, and the low voices of his guy friends.

He wore a white tee shirt that made his smile dazzling, his dark hair like midnight, his eyes like golden moons. She didn't stop at the adoring gathering but pushed past, going into the quiet of the class room.

Ms. Tingey was writing on the blackboard but she turned around when the door opened and noise filtered it. "Jenn. I'm surprised you're here."

"Why?" Jennifer dropped her books onto the desk with a thud.

"After your injury. Are you okay?"

"I just fainted."

"I heard you were out for forty minutes."

Jennifer laughed. "Try forty seconds."

Ms. Tingey shook her head and finished writing the journal entry of the day: *Resolving conflict*

Other students entered and laughter and noise from the group surrounding John lured Ms.Tingey to the door. Jennifer watched through the long glass panel in the center of the door. Ms. Tingey went to the group and was soon laughing and talking just like the rest of them.

Jennifer sat at her desk with a sigh, her eyes settling on what Ms. Tingey had written on the blackboard. Her mind swam with fantasies of John falling off the face of the earth or being lost somewhere on safari or some other such event. That would rid her life of conflict quite nicely.

When the bell shrilled the boisterous group dispersed. John came into the room behind Ms.Tingey, both of them laughing about something.

Jennifer watched him through narrowed eyes, not expecting him to do anything but plant his butt in his chair. It surprised her when the first thing he did was look at her. She pinched her lips, forbidding them to smile.

Confusion shifted on his face. He sat down. Then he mouthed something to her. She wasn't sure what it was, she was too annoyed to study his lips. If she did, she'd lose the anger and she was enjoying it too much.

"What?" she finally whispered after he'd tried twice to unobtrusively mouth a message to her.

The room went quiet.

"You okay?"

"I'm fine."

"I suppose you all heard about Jennifer's accident during opening night last night," Miss Tingey announced with all seriousness. Jennifer sat erect, pleased to have the spotlight.

"I was there," somebody said. "You'd have never known anything was wrong."

"Yeah. Way to go, Jenn." The boy sitting across from her lifted his palm and waited for her to slap it. After she did, she sat back, ready to tell her side of the story.

"An intense play." Jessica linked fingers crusted with gnarly silver rings. "I totally cried at the end when John was completely into it. You rock."

Jennifer's head jerked right. The spotlight now flashed on John. He sat casually in his chair, head dipping humbly every now and again, his cheeks infuriatingly pink. *I'm surprised he has the grace to blush,* Jennifer thought crossing her arms over her chest.

The conversation was all about John then, and Jennifer steamed. Finally, she raised her hand and Ms.Tingey called on her.

"You have to be prepared to improvise. Who knows what an unseasoned actor would do if something like that happened."

Some of the class murmured in agreement, but for the most part, the comment ended the discussion centered on John and that left Jennifer with a smirk of satisfaction.

"Journal entry for today." Ms. Tingey pointed to what she had scrawled on the board. "Five minutes and then we'll discuss it."

Jennifer quickly wrote about how she would eliminate the problem causing the conflict. Case in point, *an annoying neighbor = moving.* Her thoughts drifted to the fantasy. His family moving out, knowing she'd never have to take another rung up the ladder with John nipping at her heels.

She glanced over at him. His head tilted over the desk. He was deeply focused, writing. Jennifer was dying to know what he was writing about. What conflict would John Michaels have to deal with? his temporary lack of a vehicle? There were hundreds ready to jump at the opportunity to be seen giving John a ride anywhere. He had the usual family conflicts, even he wasn't immune to that yet it seemed to her the world and everyone in it opened their arms to him.

"So how do we do it?" Ms. Tingey perched herself on the corner of her desk. "How do we resolve conflict?" Ms. Tingey corrected herself. "Let's first look at *Pride and Prejudice* since I know you're all close to finishing it by now, right?" She held up her hands to quiet the mumblings. "How did Mr. Darcy resolve the conflict?"

"He was wealthy and socially powerful," Jennifer said. "He had everything at his disposal to make Lydia's life different, so he did."

"But he did it for Elizabeth," John added.

Their gazes locked across the room. Jennifer wondered why he chose to stare at her with a look she couldn't figure out.

"So he resolved Lydia's problems with money, something most of us don't have the luxury of." Miss Tingey walked in front of the room. "And, as Jennifer so astutely pointed out, he also used his social position. Another extra most of us don't have as part of our repertoire. What about his conflicts with Elizabeth?"

Jessica raised her hand and Ms.Tingey nodded at her. "Mr. Darcy and Elizabeth finally ditched their pride and talked it out."

"Pride was an issue for them both, wasn't it, up until the very end," Ms. Tingey said.

"There's no substitute for communication," John said. The class erupted into agreement. Jennifer looked over at him again. This time he was not looking at her.

Jennifer knew all of the cars on her street and who they belonged to. It came from having spent the last ten years living in the same house. It also came from being a girl who noticed everything, like the random car driving by with wide-eyed girls trying to nonchalantly look at John's house on a stalker cruise-by.

The fancy white Mercedes sitting in front of the Michaels' house didn't belong to anyone on the street.

Jennifer parked her car in her driveway. John's grandparents both drove Toyota's. She knew what his friends drove—and none of them drove a Mercedes. The license plate wasn't from out of state.

Her curiosity was pricked.

She found Parker at the kitchen table doing homework, dipping Oreo's in orange juice. "Where's Mom?" If anyone knew what was going on at the Michaels', it was her mother.

"Cleaning Amber up. She poured orange juice all over herself."

Snatching an Oreo out of the plastic tray, Jennifer hummed the tune they danced to in the play, seeing John's face in the corner of her mind. She took the stairs two at a time and found her mother on Amber's bedroom floor with a wet washcloth rubbing Amber's orange-stained face.

"Jefer!" Amber lifted her arms up.

"Hey, baby." Crouching down, Jennifer took her sister into her arms. Her mother stuffed the washcloth into Jennifer's palm.

"Finish, will you?" The request was more demanding

than Jennifer was used to. Her mother stood, wiping her brow with the back of her hand.

"Something wrong?" Jennifer took another swipe at Amber's face before concentrating on sticky little hands. The line between her mother's brows warned her something was up.

"The Michaels may list their house."

Jennifer's heart jumped to her throat and lodged there. Her hands, holding Amber's, froze. "Why?"

Her mother's eyes glistened. Her mother loved Janice Michaels—the women were best friends. Jennifer's heart ripped down the center with the news. She stood, clutching Amber to her hip. "Things still bad?"

Maggie nodded, tears slipping down her cheeks. "I wish there was something I could do."

Jennifer lowered Amber gently to the floor then put her arms around her mother, her own tears choking her throat. It had been financially hard for the Michaels' for some time.

Maggie eased back from her daughter's embrace and cupped her cheeks, smiling. "The stock market's so crazy. It's been hard for people to want to invest."

"But he's trustworthy," Jennifer said.

"I know, I know. It's just that nobody wants to trust the market right now. They're all pulling out, sitting back and waiting. That leaves Mitchell with very little business."

For Jennifer, it would be easier being dropped into the darkness of the ocean, rather than hear the news. Her brief fantasy of John moving out of her life vanished now with reality. She turned away so the tears she blinked back would not be seen. Her mother's warm hand went to her shoulder.

"Will they move?" The crack in Jennifer's voice gave her away. John was moving. Her mind flashed with barbecues at sunset, hours swinging from the tire swing in his back yard, Christmas parties, birthday parties, his face out her window.

"If they have to, yes."

"Where?"

"They haven't talked about it, at least not that they've told us. But they need to lower their mortgage payment."

When her mother brought her in for a hug she closed her eyes, feeling amazingly like a child, and wishing she was. Wishing she and John were children again.

"Want some dinner?" They walked arm-in-arm down to the kitchen with Amber at their heels. Jennifer's stomach hollowed. She wasn't hungry. She shook her head.

"How's the show?"

Her mother was trying to take her mind off of things, but the void in Jennifer's stomach spread to her heart. "Good."

"I can't wait to see it."

"Does everybody know? The kids?"

"I'm sure they do." Maggie's arm slipped away and she went to a cabinet and opened it. "Set the table, please."

Mechanically, Jennifer set the table. No more whispers across the yard through their windows. The clattering chug of John's old truck wouldn't announce that he was nearby. No longer would the pleasant calm of his voice drift up through her open window when he was outside doing something, anything at all.

She didn't want to eat. She had no desire to make small talk over dinner. After she finished with the table, she ran upstairs to her bedroom. She could have flung herself across her bed and sobbed, she ached inside. Instead, she paused in the door frame, staring out the window with trepidation.

John was still back at school. On her way out of the main building she saw him talking with Runt and the only other boy she'd ever seen Runt hang around besides John. She didn't even know the kid's name. But John was laughing and talking with them.

Crossing the floor to the window, she was overcome with conflicting waves, like angry tides inside of her. She'd been stupid, rude. Mean. She'd wasted time. Pride, the strongest tide of all, had sucked her into its fierce vortex and she'd let it take her under, and now it was too late.

Lowering to her bed, she sat in a daze, staring out into the darkness of his window.

She caught sight of him the next day in the hall on the way to Miss Tingey's. Of course he was surrounded by friends. To look at him now, knowing he might soon be out of her life poked a hole in her heart. She slowed as she neared, hoping he'd see her, that maybe—well, she didn't want to hope that he would sense her presence.

Loitering had never been her style, but today she waited.

The first bell rang. Those surrounding him scattered and he was left alone. He still didn't see her and she was perturbed enough to accidentally drop a book. The sound brought his attention to her. He jogged over.

She pretended she hadn't masterminded the meeting, and dropped to her knees, retrieved the book just as he dipped down at the same time. Squatting there in the hall, their eyes met. Each had a hand on her book.

He smiled as they stood. He gave her full ownership of the hardback. "You're late, Vien."

"You know me," she said.

"Yeah." They began a slow walk to Miss Tingey's room.

"Mom says you might be moving," she said.

He let out a sigh. "Yeah."

Do you feel as sad about it as me? "That's kind of exciting, I guess."

Lifting a shoulder he kept his eyes on the floor and didn't say anything.

"Are you excited? New friends, new house, new school?"

He finally looked over. "Would you want to move near the end of your senior year?"

"Guess not."

"I'd finish the year out here anyway. I'd just drive over."

"You mean when you're not grounded from the car?" she added lightly. He didn't laugh, in fact, his face tightened.

"You like it when I suffer, don't you?" he asked.

She couldn't tell if he was being funny or not, not when his eyes sharpened. "Are you—you're just joking right?"

He stopped, staring hard at her.

"I don't like seeing you..." she couldn't say the words, they sounded so ridiculous. But if that's what he thought, she was mortified. "That's stupid." She kept walking to Miss Tingey's.

"You'd be glad if we moved." He was right next to her, his shoulder brushing hers.

"That is so not true. You're way off base."

"How off base?"

"What do you mean?"

"That's a leading answer, Jenn. I have to know the reason for it. How wrong am I? How off base?"

"I'm not going to answer that."

"Won't or can't?"

The challenge in his eyes stopped her. This was supposed to be about him moving. *How did it get twisted around to me? I'm losing my edge.*

"Guess you can't," he said. A little triumph mixed with disappointment in his voice. "Figured." He strode off ahead of her.

She watched the way his confident stride taunted. Even that she liked about him. Even that she'd miss.

FOURTEEN

Everybody was off. The music didn't cue up when it was supposed to, leaving the citizens of Verona with blank faces. Somebody dropped a rapier. John forgot four lines, Andrew one. Trish, who played the nurse, tripped during three of her entrances, sending the audience into a laugh with each one, changing the tone of the play to slapstick.

Chip blew a fuse during intermission, sweating, growling, pacing like a terrier in a junkyard. They gathered in the drama room. "We've done this too many times for these kinds of tricks to be happening, guys," he said.

No one dared speak. Standing like the VonTrapp children, they took the chastisement from their father.

"Ty, the music—it sucked big time."

"Sorry." Head bowed, Ty nodded. "Won't happen again, Chief."

"Our audience isn't sure if this is a comedy or what," Chip snapped, stopping directly in front of Trish. "Watch your step." Timidly she nodded.

Chip moved to John. At first, he just stared at him. John kept his head up, eyes steady. Jennifer watched, her heart swollen for him. She hoped Chip wouldn't say anything to hurt him.

"You should have improvised."

"I know."

"You know this stuff, I know you do."

"I'm sorry."

"I've seen you improvise before, with brilliance in fact."

"I'm sorry."

"Improvise."

John gave a sharp nod.

Chip turned to everyone. Rather than say anything more, he left the room with the thickness of rebuke in the air. It took a while to breathe. Quietly, cautiously, the cast moved, some settling into seats, others pacing, repeating lines.

Jennifer's gaze followed John as he found a spot alone. Lacey, Fletcher and Andrew headed toward him but he held out a hand to keep them from coming near and shook his head. He set his hands on the wall, as if pressing against it. The full shirt he wore didn't disguise the tenseness riding his back and shoulders. There was more setting on those shoulders than anybody in the room knew and Jennifer suddenly found herself going to him. Maybe he'd stop her too, but his hands never left the wall, as if he alone held it up.

He looked at her. She inched close so they wouldn't be overheard. "You okay?" she whispered.

Flecks of color in his eyes changed. He stood back, his hands dropping to his sides.

He didn't think anything could ease the storm raging inside, but when he heard movement behind him, his heart dared hope it was Jennifer. She looked up through eyes bright, earnest, and understanding.

As kids they'd tried to read each others' minds and

had been frustrated when they couldn't. He had to open his mouth and talk to her—tell her what he was feeling inside. Mr.Darcy and his stubborn pride came to his mind. He wanted to laugh, knew it would feel good to. She'd laugh too, if he told her.

She stood close. The side of his arm was dangerously close to her breast. He swallowed and looked at a scarred poster of "West Side Story" that had hung on the wall for too many years. The yellow in the words faded to an eerie sallow shade.

He forgot four lines tonight. Four. Four he knew backwards and upside down. He shook his head, worked to search his mind for what he'd done well in the performance. But his father's face, fraught with worry, that card with Coldwell Banker Realty on it he'd found next to the phone, blocked everything.

"Want to run lines?" she asked.

The pressure inside gave just enough that he could breathe. Just stay here with me, he wanted to say. And so much more, but that was too much.

When she brushed against his arm, his veins coursed with bubbles.

"Sure you're okay?" she asked, resting her hand on his arm. He nodded, glad she saw something and asked, pleased to feel her touch.

Her hair was in pale-lemon ringlets cascading everywhere. Her cheeks flushed. A light glistening shone on her skin but her lips were completely naked—totally kissable. He forced his eyes from them, back to the faded words "West Side Story."

They had their death scene yet. He'd kiss her then, taste her then. Feel her body against his. His blood rammed through every part of him, settling in his abdomen.

Get your head on straight, Michaels.

It was almost time for the second act, and for the fight with Andrew. *Good.* He needed something and a cold shower was not an option.

"Good luck." Her whisper was warm in his ear, the light touch on his arm nearly paralyzing.

"It's time." Ty's voice cut the quiet like the tick of a clock in a tomb.

John stole another look at Jennifer's face. He had to pull himself up and out of this depressive rut fast or he'd drag the show down. It would only take one thing to make his spirit, certainly his body, forget. His gaze skipped over her face with eyes hungry for more than just a look. This was not the place, not the time for what he wanted. He'd get through the night because he wanted what tomorrow might bring.

John rode through the second half of the play ready to explode with energy. Every line was right on, every cue met, and he ran with his instincts when he and Jennifer kissed. They'd brought whistles and screams from the audience, but he'd been too deep into Romeo to allow himself the perk of truly enjoying the kisses.

He couldn't stand still offstage. He didn't want to fall from whatever inertial track he was on by chatting mindlessly while he waited for his cues, so he kept to himself, sword in hand, his heart chugging in anticipation.

He wanted to please Chip, himself—everybody in

fact—with the rest of the night's performance. It was his job as Romeo, leader and star.

Jennifer did her part.

He saw her whispering pep talks; patting everybody as they exited the stage after scenes. She even smiled at him from across the stage earlier. He smiled back, but didn't let his look linger, worried looking at her when he wasn't in character would break the perfect bubble they seemed to be playing in.

She was on stage now, hidden in the tomb. The edges of her dress peeked out from the shadow. Juliet waiting in the tomb for her love. His throat tightened. Something about the idea caused sensation to swell inside of him.

Jennifer, waiting—for me.

Soon, Romeo would take up his sword again in defense of his love. John's mind rolled the dialogue, readying to step onto the stage. Taking the rapier in both hands, his fingers slid along the narrow, round length to the tiny bulb at the end.

Then it was time.

"This is that banished Montague that murdered my love's cousin, with which grief it is supposed the fair creature died." Paris drew his sword, aimed it directly at Romeo. "Can vengeance be pursued further than death? Condemned villain, I do apprehend thee. Obey and go with me, for thou must die."

Steel challenged steel, slicing through the air like ministers of death, demanding the audience be silent. The giant room went still with only the sounds of breath heaving and feet scraping. Sweat flew through the lights like strings of broken beads.

Romeo forced Paris up the stairs, the two of them perilously dancing near the edge, the rapiers streaming through the air meeting with a clattering. Gasps fluttered up from the audience like wafts of smoke. A hearty round of applause broke through the breathy noises coming from the stage, as if some of the tension building in the room would ease. It didn't.

John carefully took the stairs backward, one-by-one as Andrew forced him down. Sweat dripped, stinging his eyes. His heart thundered in his chest. Before he knew it, his body took an extra swing—one they hadn't choreographed.

Andrew's eyes opened wide only momentarily, as the blade skimmed the sleeve of his shirt, ripping. They both paused, shocked. A strange surge of power and need for revenge filled John, for Romeo.

Romeo lunged, thrusting his weapon one last time into Paris, sending his adversary to his death.

"Oh, I am slain!" Paris choked. *"If thou be merciful, open the tomb. Lay me with Juliet."*

Romeo stood triumphantly over Paris, his breath heaving in and out, sweat tracking down the angles of his face and onto his neck. *"In faith, I will."*

John wiped his brow and gulped in air, continuing the next lengthy monologue without a break.

As he knelt over Jennifer, words flowed without effort or thought. He reached under her body, stole a seconds pleasure from holding her limp in his arms and squeezed her next to him.

"Ah, dear Juliet! Why art thou yet so fair? Shall I believe that unsubstantial death is amorous and that the lean abhorred monster keeps thee here in the dark to be

his paramour?"

He wept again, readily. Salty tears streamed down his cheeks. He bent his head, readying for the kiss.

"Will I set up my everlasting rest, and shake the yoke of inauspicious stars from this world-wearied flesh. Eyes, look your last. Arms, take your last embrace. And lips, O you the doors of breath, seal with a righteous kiss, a dateless bargain to engrossing death."

The audience was silent, like mourners in a graveyard. His own cries echoed off the walls of the auditorium and filled his head. Tears choked his throat.

He kissed her.

When he pulled back, his tears stained her mouth. *"O true apothecary, they drugs are quick. Thus with a kiss I die."*

After the last curtain call, the cast scurried out front to meet and greet. John searched for Andrew and found him laughing with Lacey.

"You okay?" he asked.

Andrew held up his arm where a clean rip in the sleeve proved John's handiwork with the rapier. John's gut twisted. "I'm sorry."

"No problem, dude. Nothing happened. But Chip may have your butt for wrecking the costume."

John didn't want to think about what could have happened had he taken a chunk out of Andrew's arm with the rapier.

"You were awesome, by the way," Andrew said.

"So perfect," Lacey piped, threading her arm in John's. "Were you actually crying? That was beyond cool."

John wet his lips and started toward the auditorium

lobby like Chip had directed. He glanced over his shoulder hoping to see where Jennifer was.

Andrew patted John on the back. "And the Oscar goes to..."then he was dragged away by Fletcher, who led him in the direction of a group of waiting friends.

Lacey still had his arm, and John glanced down at it wondering how he could get out of the lock gracefully. He spotted Jennifer with her parents and his parents and gently pulled his arm free of Lacey's.

"There's my parents." He started toward them, and Lacey followed.

"Oh, cool. I'd like to meet them."

John joined the group mid-conversation and stood next to Jennifer. She radiated in her burgundy dress. Soft curls framed her glowing cheeks and brought the blue out in her eyes.

"You were wonderful," Maggie said, hugging her.

"Great job." Randy embraced her too.

Maggie looked at him next. "That fight scene looked so real, John. Like the movies."

"Great special effects," Randy added.

Jennifer's heart pounded. She still tasted John's tears. She hadn't had the chance to tell him what she thought of their death scene. Perfect.

Janice Michaels glowed. "You were wonderful. Both of you."

Mitchell nodded in agreement. "I said to Jan, I can't believe that's our little Jenn Vien up there."

"Their chemistry," her dad grinned, "sizzled."

"Convincing," Mitchell put in. "Your expertise and training has paid off, Jenn."

"And John was great," Randy added.

"Jennifer was the star," Mitchell made the point. "She's earned it." He didn't even look at John. Jennifer's heart dropped. No compliment for John's outstanding performance?

"I still can't believe that was John." Her dad spoke up. "You were something else."

John hid disappointment well, Jennifer thought, closely watching the expression on his face.

"Thanks, Randy."

"Memorization has always been a challenge for him," Mitchell put in. "Chip told us you took a swing that wasn't choreographed."

John stared at his dad. Jennifer tried to read the silent message being sent through angry eyes, but couldn't.

John's feelings were ignored then as her parents and his said their goodbyes and left. Jennifer's heart swelled for him. He continued to talk and laugh with the other cast members, but she knew his face too well. The cordial mask he wore didn't disguise that he was still thinking about his dad's negligence.

Lacey's flirty laugh broke the air like a howling saxophone. She walked up to John with her mother at her side. Unabashedly, she hooked her arm in his again. "Party at my house, John. You'll come, right?"

"You and Lace should go out sometime." Ann reached a painted nail to his shoulder and tapped. "You're such a cutie."

"Yeah, why don't we, John? I'd love to go out with you."

"Oh, don't blush, honey." Ann clacked on a piece of gum. "That makes you even cuter."

Jennifer's blood steamed.

Ann looked over. "Hi, Jenny." When Ann waved at her, her bracelets jangled. "It's my patient. How ya doing, honey?"

"Great." Jennifer joined them, annoyed John was now surrounded by three females. More annoyed that she was one of them. But she didn't want to leave him alone with these two hyenas.

The faceted colors in his eyes flecked with ambers, pale yellows and greens. Beautiful eyes, Jennifer thought, glad there seemed to be no trace of disappointment in them now, only something curious she was trying to figure out.

Ann rambled on, "I told Lace that she and John should go out. He's such a cutie."

Jennifer tried to keep her voice even. "Yes, well, Lacey knows she'd have to take a number. Right Lacey?"

Ann's laugh came out somewhere between a cackle and a whistle. "Well, I can believe it."

She patted her flowered bag, shaking her head. "Take my word for it John, it isn't gonna get any better than my Lace." She wrapped an arm around Lacey's shoulder and Lacey lowered her dark lashes. "Always judge a girl by her mama. Cause what her mama is, is what she's gonna be." She stuck both her hands out to her sides with a quick dip of her knees. "And look at me."

This was unbelievable. And neither mother nor daughter was at all embarrassed. Jennifer looked at John standing like a prisoner in the small circle, his throat constricting as if trying to say something. But it was impossible to follow up a tacky moment like this with anything dignified.

"She's very lucky," he said.

Jennifer couldn't believe John had the presence of mind to think it, let alone say the words, when all she wanted to do was dump buckets of cold water on Lacey and Ann and tell them to get over themselves.

Ann searched the crowd like a cat for a mouse. "I'm gonna go find Mr. Chips." Her fingers wrapped around Lacey's cheeks and she squeezed, then planted a kiss on Lacey's pursed lips. "Be careful, sweetie. See you at the partae, Johnny. Bye Jenny!" She turned, the *Juicy* embroidered across her backside swung with every step.

Lacey hooked her arm in John's. "I live at 483 North Locust. Ever been on my street?"

"Never have."

Lacey tugged John in the direction of the doors. "That's okay, I can show you how to get there. You can give me a ride, how's that?"

Jennifer rolled her eyes.

Jennifer almost didn't go to the party, so infuriated with Lacey and Ann and with John for not shoving Lacey away. But why would he push away a dark, tantalizing vixen like Lacey? No red-blooded male would.

She parked in Lacey's driveway. Too bad if it was considered presumptuous—John's truck was there. They were probably inside snuggling on a couch in some dark corner. Lacey was probably dropping strawberries into his mouth or blowing her breath in his face to cool him off.

Sniffling, Jennifer passed his car, saw his student council jacket neatly folded on the back seat and stopped. She gave a quick look around to make certain she was alone. Noise pulsating from the house meant most everyone coming to the party was already inside.

She opened the door of John's car and smelled the faint scent he showered in. Her tongue nervously grazed her teeth. Plucking the jacket from the back seat, a delicious chill of mischief skittered down her spine. The jacket was soft. She brought it to her nose and inhaled, an involuntary smile filling her face.

Music blasted from the house, something about Stacey's mom. She heard the voices inside singing along, but changing the words to 'Lacey's mom'.

Hmm, figures.

Jennifer slipped on the jacket and comfort infused her every pore. She ran her palms against the soft leather sleeves, taking in another deep breath of him, and closed her eyes. How many times had she dreamed of wearing this coat? He wore it everywhere. She'd never seen any other girl wear it. That was nice. Not that wearing a boy's letter jacket at Pleasant View High School meant anything. It didn't. That was an old tradition. Jennifer would have loved everyone to see her wearing John's jacket—loved it. She almost started laughing.

She would have, but she sensed she wasn't alone.

Her heart pounded. She froze. She didn't dare open her eyes; it was embarrassing for anyone to find her. But one person in particular meant wrist-slitting humiliation.

When he cleared his throat, her pounding heart dropped to her feet. She opened her eyes, turned and looked right into John's. It was the first time that night she'd seen his face light, caught somewhere between happy and intrigued.

"I was cold," she offered.

His brows lifted over eyes that said, "Uh-huh." But he didn't say anything. He reached behind her, coming close enough that their bodies touched, and pushed the car door shut. Then he stayed there. So close, Jennifer was forced to look up at him, her eyes blinking fast, her heart beating even faster. Her face was hot. She was sure it was red.

"You're welcome to wear it." The kindness in his tone melted her insides into marshmallow. She expected him to tease her. But his eyes were void of anything confrontational or condemning.

"Thanks."

"You coming in?" He still hadn't moved. His body heat began to warm her. She looked over his shoulder at the house. Somebody peered out the window, watching. Then there were two.

"You leaving?" she asked.

"I needed some air. It's suffocating in there."

The living room window filled with silhouettes, all with noses pressed to the window. The music of Stacey's mom wound down. Something slow and sweet came on—one of her favorite songs.

"I won't need the jacket inside then, will I?" Jennifer said, fantasizing about a slow dance.

"Wear it. It looks good on you."

"It does?"

He nodded. They took the path to the front door slow and easy. The shadows in the window disappeared. Through sheer drapes Jennifer saw couples locked together in a slow dance. The song, her chance, was slipping away.

He reached for the door. If she didn't ask now some other girl would take him, stealing her opportunity to dance with him to her favorite song.

"I love this song," she blurted.

He paused, listening. The words were romantic and poignant. Serious words about being a hero. Their eyes met. Her heart opened, ripping wide. She wanted him to step inside of her heart so she knew for certain he was hers.

"You did great tonight," she told him. "I didn't get to tell you."

"You were the one who was awesome," he said. "Amazing."

His compliment thrilled her. She opened her mouth to ask him for that dance when the door flung open. They were bathed in light.

"There you are." Lacey looked Jennifer over only momentarily before setting her smile on John. She reached for his sleeve. "Hurry, I want to dance with you to this song."

FIFTEEN

Jennifer refused to watch Lacey dance with John, the skank's arms so tight around his neck they could have cut off his circulation. Serves him right, she scoffed under her breath. For a flash, she hoped he'd choke and die. She put on her thespian smile and flitted from one person to the next, ignoring the dull ache in her heart.

Everyone did double takes, and she couldn't figure out why. She'd made sure her makeup was perfect, her nose free of anything offensive. And she wasn't wearing any lip gloss, so she knew it wasn't smeared or crooked.

"Hey." Fletcher poked her in the ribs.

"Fletch."

He popped a handful of M and M's from a nearby candy dish into his mouth, then rubbed his palms back and forth. Andrew and Drake bounded up behind him, smiling at her. All three eyed her curiously, then Andrew asked, "Where's John?"

Jennifer shrugged. "Somewhere." She made herself not look over, not see if John was fine, dancing with Lacey. For some reason, when her head turned anyway, the sight didn't bug her as much as she thought it would.

"Wanna dance?" Fletcher asked. "I mean, is it okay?"

"Why wouldn't it be?" Jennifer hooked her arm in his and followed him to the small area where furniture was pushed back so everybody could dance.

Something inside of her settled. Gone was the turmoil she normally carried. She and Fletcher talked about the night's performance while they shook and shimmied. She kept watch on John, on who he was with. But those strangling feelings of jealousy she'd carried for so long weren't there anymore.

John's attention stayed with her. She liked that, and smiled at him. Her heart carefully crept open.

Once, he jerked his head toward the dance area, wordlessly suggesting they meet and dance, but she was grabbed by somebody and when she searched for him again he'd been snagged by Lacey's mom who cornered him into a dance of her own.

Later, Jennifer found Lacey coming out of the powder room. "This is so much fun," she said "Great idea, having us all over."

"Thanks." They stood awkwardly in the darkened hall. Lacey's eyes honed in on the name on the jacket. "How can you be cold? It's hot in here."

"I'm not cold."

"Then let me take your jacket." Lacey stuck out her hand. "I'll just put it in the bedroom.

Jennifer wrapped her arms around the soft leather of John's jacket and shook her head. Disappointment mixed with envy on Lacey's face. "No thanks." Jennifer turned to go but Lacey stopped her.

"Did he give that to you?"

A smile crept on Jennifer's lips. "He did, as a matter of fact."

Ann relinquished John to Lacey, then danced her way around the food table where an impressive spread of chips, dips, salsa and cookies was laid out. Jennifer would have sworn this whole party-thing had been planned, rather than spontaneous.

Jennifer reached into the potato chip bowl.

"Hey, there she is." Ann waved, her body didn't stop bopping to the beat. Jennifer waved back. Ann wrapped her in a squishy hug. Jennifer's nostrils were assaulted by the smell of burnt flowers and spice. "Glad you came, honey." Standing back, Ann eyed Jennifer from head to toe and her right brow lifted. "What's this you're wearing? Are you and he?"

Jennifer noticed that some of the cast snacking at the food table quieted, listening. She took a deep breath, was ready to speak when Taunia appeared with Trish.

"Is that what I think it is?" Trish pulled on the hem of the jacket, exposing John's embroidered name. She gasped. "It is."

Everyone snacking suddenly turned to her. Voices. Giggles. More gasps, whispers.

"I can't believe it."

"Me either."

"I had no idea they were—"

"I thought she liked Alex Jesperson."

"They broke up."

"Seriously?"

"But I can't believe John gave her his jacket. That's like—"

"I know."

Ann Naeverson's heels clacked on the tile floor of the kitchen, her arms waved excitedly. "How cute it looks on you, Jenny." She tugged here and flattened there as the crowd thickened around them. Voices rose.

Excitement rang like bells. Every time Jennifer opened her mouth to explain, she was turned, elbowed or hugged by some well-wisher like a bride after vows.

"You should have said something," Ann talked over the noise. "Here I was thinking John was on the vine and you plucked him already."

Jennifer's clammy hands clutched the unzipped edges of John's coat. She hadn't plucked anybody. And when she saw John zigzagging through the crowd toward the action, she started to sweat.

He was congratulated for something he was clueless about; his face fraught with congenial confusion. She wanted to run. With her eye on Lacey's back door, she began a stealthy escape, but the room was so packed she couldn't move.

"Hey." It was John. Jennifer pretended she didn't hear him. He whistled a sharp, ballpark whistle she hadn't heard since childhood. The sound cut through the noise like a rapier through cloth, leaving the thud of the sound system with Maroon Five asking if there was anyone out there.

"Jenn."

"I'm going out back for some air." Jennifer headed for the door.

"Turn on that light," Ann called. "It's darker than a bar in broad daylight out there."

Jennifer let out a sigh the minute she was out the door. She would have enjoyed the cool night air, the freedom from the embarrassing moment, but she hadn't turned on the light and she didn't know about the two cement steps. She landed on her stomach in a flat thud. Her arms broke the fall, protecting her face from grinding the rest of her to a stop. She laid in the dark in what looked like a basic yoga position before the light flicked on and John was at her side.

"You okay?"

"Sure. Yeah. I am."

His hands wrapped around her arms to help her and she scrambled up with as much dignity she could. Brushing off his jacket kept her face and eyes averted. Her cheeks heated to fire.

"I'm not sure your jacket is, though." The leather of the sleeves was scraped. "I'm sorry."

"It's okay."

"I'll have it cleaned for you." She couldn't brush off the jacket forever, but she was afraid to look at him. She headed for the door. After that humiliating fall, she was ready to split the party for good. His palm wrapped around her elbow.

"Just a second," he said. "Can I talk to you for a minute?"

When she finally had the courage to meet his gaze, she was surprised that he didn't look upset.

"Okay."

He stuffed his hands in the front pockets of his jeans. "I heard something inside."

"Oh?" Her heart flickered a little. She reached for the zipper of the coat, fumbled with it.

"Everybody thinks you and I...that you and me—"It was hard to say the words and John stopped because she was grinning, like she was teasing him.

"This is the first time I've seen you flustered," she said.

"I'm not flustered," he lied. He was so nervous his hands were shaking, had been since he'd escaped to the front yard and found her wearing his coat.

It was the last thing he expected to find: Jennifer in his car putting on his coat. The look on her face when she'd slipped on the jacket had stopped him in his tracks. Something powerful had stirred his system. She looked great in it. The light sleeves played off the pale blonde in her hair, lit now by moonlight. He didn't think her sea-blue eyes could look any bluer, but they did. Dark and deep, like the mysterious zenith of the sky.

"Inside," he cleared his throat, trying again. "Everybody said that you said we were, you know."

"What?"

"That—"

"You'll have to say it John. I'm not going to say it for you."

His toes crinkled in his shoes, his hands twitched in his pockets. *Why did she do this to him? Make him feel like he wanted to say everything in his heart but at the same time make it hard?*

"I guess everybody thinks," he gestured to the coat with a nod of his head, "with you wearing my coat and stuff."

Her teasing smile faded. Slowly, she eased out of the jacket. Then she carefully folded it over her arm and extended it to him. "Sorry. Here."

He took the jacket even though he didn't want it back. "You can still wear it if you want, if you're cold."

"I'm not." But her arms went around her middle. "Thanks, though."

"Jenn." He almost stopped her. Instead, he watched her go back into the house. How could he be the one to say it? That everybody thought they were together. Even if he wished it was true, telling her meant letting down his guard first. He was afraid to do that.

She was probably joking when she told everybody about the jacket—making him look like some home-boy, all chivalrous and starry-eyed with the gesture. His fingers squeezed the coat. The fabric was still warm. He brought it to his nose and inhaled. Before the warmth vanished, he slipped it on.

John hung the coat on a knob in his bedroom—the old knob his mom had installed when he'd gone through his baseball phase. The miniature bat and ball were scuffed and worn looking now.

Something heavy clamped over his heart. For a moment he stood in his bedroom, didn't move, didn't think. He didn't want to. Everybody liked the performance, even with the lame first act, his four lost lines, and the accidents in the second half. He'd given his soul to Romeo. And everyone had complimented him.

Except his dad.

A vein of resentment hardened inside. He pulled off his shirt, twisted it and tossed it into his closet—missing the laundry basket. In three strides he picked it up and shoved it deep into the nearly-stuffed container. He had the sudden urge to lift the basket over his head and toss its contents all over his room.

He kicked at it instead, setting his hands on his hips with an exasperated growl.

No matter what he did it was never enough.

He fell on the bed, scrubbing his hands over his

face, old frustration boiling. Times like this he cocooned his self image with what few memories he had of when he'd made his dad proud. The memories were always right at the edge of his thoughts. He'd used them so many times. Like when he'd mowed the Vienvu's lawn because Randy had been gone for three weeks. "I'm proud of you." His dad had looked at him with such pride that John felt security wrap around his bones.

His bones ached tonight. He was ready to dissolve into the mattress. The darkness out his window made him feel empty. He liked it when he saw light in Jennifer's bedroom.

He'd miss that.

He'd never thought much about possessions. They'd go with him when they moved; it was what he couldn't take that hollowed his heart. If moving was inevitable, he'd do it and try not to show how hard it was.

"John?" His dad knocked on the door.

John shot up, rubbing away any sign of misery from his face. "Yeah?"

His dad only took one step into the room. John didn't know if he was showing respect for his space or silently telling him he wasn't going to stay long.

"How was the party?"

John shrugged. "Okay I guess."

A moment of silence stretched into two, three. John waited, anxious, not sure what to expect. Disappointment hung in his chest when his dad turned, and went out the door.

The aching in John's bones intensified, the very marrow burning. After his dad shut the door, he crawled into bed and stared out the window.

Jennifer walked down the crowded hall to English. More strangers said hello to her, more boys smiled. Fame was intoxicating. To be noticed, adored, what girl wouldn't like it?

Romeo and Juliet played to a packed house every night. Chip was ecstatic. Nightly standing ovations, cheers, screams, were expected. But the most outrageous so far was the bra some girl had thrown up on stage when John was taking his bow. That'll go down in Pleasant View High School history, Jennifer mused, picturing John's face when he warily plucked the black, lacey garment off the stage. He'd turned the color of beets.

John's laugh trickled through the hall now. The luring sound made Jennifer's head turn as she approached Ms.Tingey's room. She peeked in the open door. John stood talking to Ms.Tingey like they were old friends, not teacher and student.

When she went in, both of them turned.

"Jenn," Ms. Tingey smiled. "I was just hearing about the behind-the-scene antics. I can't believe I haven't seen the show and tonight's closing night."

Jennifer set her books on her desk. "Can't you come?"

"Hey, do you have any tickets left?" John asked. Obviously, he assumed she'd sold all of hers. *What a joke.*

"I do, actually." Jennifer dug into her backpack.

"Oh, good." Miss Tingey retrieved her purse. "Do you have more than one?"

Jennifer wanted to whisper that she had seven, knowing John had sold his, but she just handed the stack to him. "You sell them to her."

He looked at her outstretched hand. "No way, you do it."

"You've already won the contest."

John put his hands up. "They're yours, you do it."

"But you've already sold more. You do it."

Ms.Tingey laughed. "I heard about the contest. The winner gets what, a day off school? I'll take them all. I have friends who want to come." She tucked them into her purse, pulled out her checkbook and began to write.

Jennifer looked at John. "So, how does it feel to be getting a day off? Congratulations."

John shifted, plunging his hands into his front pockets. "I'm not much for contests."

Jennifer laughed. "Since when?" The door opened and a few students filed in. "Or have you forgotten that you used to trip me when we raced?"

He turned away, pretending, she thought, to look at who had just come in because his face was red. Cute.

"Dude, that's like, bad to trip a girl." Freddy overheard Jennifer's comment as he plunked himself into his seat.

"We were kids." John went to his desk and sat, but his eyes held Jennifer's, and behind them something mischievous glinted.

"Here you go, Jenn." Miss Tingey handed Jennifer the check. "I can't wait to see it. And John, I guess you'll have to share the sale with Jennifer."

"You rock, dude." Freddy slapped John's palm.

"I didn't win," John said again as the class filled,

each student anxious for the buzz of what was going on.

Jennifer wasn't mad that he won. That was like being mad at Robin Hood for giving to the poor.

"Okay." Miss Tingey took the attention of the class with one clap of her hands. "Today's journal entry is coming to terms with denial and acceptance. I want real thought put into this one everyone. Be ready for a deep discussion."

The class fell quiet. Jennifer looked at her blank paper. A trickling discomfort began to spread through her. This was not one of her strengths, denial and acceptance.

"Like, denying what?" Freddy asked, stumped.

Behind him, Jessica raised her hand, fingernails painted black. "Like self denial. As in, I want another tattoo on my rear and I know I can't afford it. That's self denial."

The class murmured. Jessica shrugged and Freddy muttered, "Good thing she ran outta money."

"You seen my butt lately?" Jessica asked, throwing the class into jests.

"I'm talking about denial in the sense that Elizabeth denied she had any feelings for Mr. Darcy other than contempt and visa versa," Miss Tingey explained. "Until they both accepted their true feelings they both experienced a form of denial. What are you in denial about? What do you need to accept? That's what this journal entry is about. Write, write."

Should I just write John's name on the paper and be done with it? That would just about say it all, Jennifer thought. He was writing so intensely. *What could he be in denial about? The move?* That idea didn't settle well in her heart.

How about that the play will be over tonight?

No, that sounds more like me. No more fans, no more compliments. Forever gone will be the fun backstage, the hours of tiring, yet satisfying and challenging rehearsals. Lines, once impossible to secure in the brain will begin to fade.

That sounds more like me.

She so wanted to read his journal entries, really see inside his head. Thievery was not her career of choice however. She had other ways.

She raised her hand, waiting for Ms.Tingey to notice. The teacher had her back to the class, and Jennifer almost lost her nerve, but Freddy cleared his throat, bringing Ms. Tingey around.

"Jenn?"

"How about we all share something?"

Bodies shifted in seats, some sat perfectly still at the suggestion. Ms.Tingey glowed. Score. Jennifer hoped she'd lit the flame of competition in John so he'd unwittingly share something he'd written down.

"Excellent, daring suggestion, Jennifer. Excellent. Why don't you start?"

I'm an actress, Jennifer reminded herself. "Sure," she said confidently. "I've been in denial about the play ending. It's been so great. I've made so many friends. I keep thinking it can't end."

"Or what?" Ms. Tingey asked.

"Or I'll be depressed, sad." Jennifer sat back, pleased with her delivery. It wasn't what was deeply hidden in her heart, but it was truth.

"Why?" John asked out of nowhere.

Jennifer's heart skipped. "I just said why, because I'll miss everyone. I've made a lot of friends."

"But you had all of those friends to begin with," he pointed out. "There's another reason."

She froze. Her heart thudded heavily. "If there is, then you tell me."

The room grew still. Heads turned first to Jennifer, then to John. His expression shifted from skepticism to determination.

"You wanted something from it," he began. "Something you're still not sure you're going to get."

Her thrumming heart beat in her throat. "I did?"

He nodded. "That's what you're in denial about."

"What did you want?" Jessica asked.

The class whispered. It was her own fault he'd pinned her down like this. She was the one to open the discussion. Jennifer thought a flickering of hope lit John's eyes.

"All right, I'll admit, I wanted something. But I could see it wasn't going to happen. So I've gone from denial to acceptance."

His face changed quickly, the glint of hope darkened with what she thought was disappointment. Turning forward, he looked at the board.

"That's it?" Jessica complained. "That's conveniently vague."

"What about you? It's your turn, John," Jennifer egged.

Heads aimed anxiously John's direction. His fingers played with the paper he was writing on, his eyes were downcast there as well. "I'm in denial, sure."

Jennifer's pulse thrummed. He looked ready to

unload something of grave importance. Her dreams and fantasies were ready to run with what it might be.

"Because of?" Jessica sneered. "Which girl to turn down this weekend?" The suggestion was harsh, but it broke the tension building in the room, and John laughed a little. But then his jaw hardened, his gaze fixed again on the paper in his hands as if it would bring him strength or give him the answer. "I'm in denial about moving," he said quietly. The admission was followed by soft whispers.

"But I don't have to be in denial about it because, even if we do move, I can still finish my life here." Freddy lightly slugged John's arm. Others turned in their seats, relieved John Michaels was not going to leave.

Jennifer's eyes met his. A gush of pleasure coursed through her body and brought a small smile to her face. His relieved expression stayed fixed on her.

SIXTEEN

They stood in a circle, shoulders tight, hands clasped, heads bowed as Chip gave his final encouraging words for the last performance. John's heart was heavy, there was no ignoring it. Jennifer wasn't the only one in denial about the play ending.

She stood close, but not right next to him. He wished he was next to her and could take her hand for this. But he was still uncertain inside. She was so aloof, so hard to read. That smile in class this afternoon was sweet. But he'd seen her smile that same way at dozens of guys.

"Break a leg," Chip said. The good luck phrase was a theater tradition. Cast members hugged.

When Jennifer turned from hugging Fletcher, John's palms moistened. She looked up at him. Around them prop people buzzed and cast members took their starting positions. She seemed to wait for him to make the first move.

John took a deep breath and extended his arms. Was that hesitation in her stance? He almost snapped his arms back, feeling stupid. But suddenly she pressed against him, all warm and soft. He lowered his face to her hair, took in a breath. Absently, his hand moved to her back. "Good luck, Jenn."

Her arms closed tight around him. "You too."

"Two households, both alike in dignity in fair Verona where we lay our scene, from ancient grudge break to new mutiny, where civil blood makes civil hands unclean From forth the fatal loins of these two foes a pair of star-crossed lovers take their life, whose misadventured piteous overthrows, doth with their death bury their parents' strife. The fearful passage of death-marked love and the continuance of their parents' rage, which, but their children's end, naught could remove, Is now the two hours' traffic of our stage – the which, if you with patient ears attend, what here shall miss, our toil shall strive to mend."

John never looked out at the audience. He'd learned that if he did, the fragile bubble holding his concentration popped; causing him to forget his lines and fumble his moves.

There was something comfortingly anonymous about the sea of heads floating in the darkened room that made performing easier. He knew there was an audience; he enjoyed it when they laughed. It almost stole his voice when he heard sniffling, knowing somehow he touched their souls. That was still a secret miracle to him. He was just John Michaels. Yet he'd made somebody feel something inside that moved them to tears. It was humbling, empowering and completely unfathomable.

If only he could figure out how to move Jennifer.

Things went perfectly in the first act. Only one mike scrabbled out and it was fixed instantly by the tech crew.

Everybody was high on adrenalin, stretching out the moments, hoping to make them last forever even though they all knew they couldn't. At intermission, John decided to take another daring step.

He found Jennifer touching up her makeup at the makeup table. The lights surrounding the mirror lit her skin to ivory and cream, as if she sat in front of an altar at church. The room was a mad house of noise, but he shoved it out of his mind.

He came up behind her, stood in the light with her. Everything inside of him swelled, urging him to do something. The show was almost over. Just one hour, and all he hoped the show would bring to him—to them, would be gone.

Her blue eyes locked on his. She stopped dabbing the fluffy powder at her chin.

"What?" she asked.

"Today in class," he began. "You were holding back."

Her eyes widened. He'd hit the mark. He waited. Slowly she put the fluffy puff back into the round, white box that held powder.

"Okay. Maybe I was."

"Why?"

"Why do you want to know?"

"Because I think I already know."

"Then you tell me."

He shook his head. "Not this time, Jenn. You say it."

She smiled a little, slid out of the chair and stood in front of him. "I'd rather hear what you *think* I'm going to say."

His lips eased into a grin. He shook his head. "Not

this time. I want to hear you say it."

She seemed to consider him. His heart raced. His fingers opened and closed. If he could tear the answer out of her, he would. *Tell me. Tell me now and put me out of my misery.* But her smile only deepened with that aloof, secretive sparkle she wore. Something magical he knew he'd never touch, never know. A bittersweet misery engulfed him, one he wished he could put her through.

"Fine," he sighed, then looked around with feigned disinterest, just to see where it got him. Out the corner of his eye her smile wilted like a dry daisy. "Well," he kept his voice cool. "See you on stage."

"Five minutes!" Ty called at the door, warning them that intermission was almost over. John wanted to turn around and look at Jennifer so badly he almost did. Instead, he interrupted a game of cards going full swing between Andrew, Fletcher, and Drake.

"This game won't end before we go on," Andrew said, eyes tight on his cards. "What'll we do?"

"We'll continue it, no matter what," Drake told him. The boys all agreed. John knew it was in hopes of keeping even a thread of the production strung together after the play ended. He grabbed a chair, turned it around and straddled it, watching.

Then he felt a tap at his shoulder.

"Can I talk to you for a second?"

Casually, he looked up into Jennifer's perturbed face. "Sure." Pleasure lifted his lips into a grin. He trailed her to the only empty corner of the drama room. She was thinking. *Good.* He wanted her to say the words, just like she always insisted that he say them. So he forced her back deep into the corner.

Her blue eyes darted around, as if she was achingly uncomfortable. He didn't care. He was ready to see her squirm.

"Okay," she whispered.

He leaned close, his hand cupping his hear. "Excuse me, did you say something?"

She could have started a fire with the blaze in her eyes. She wasn't really mad at him, but there was the undeniable familiar pleasure of the fight, making everything in his system jitter.

"I don't know what you think I'm going to say, but—"

"Come on," he started, frustration surfacing.

"Okay, okay." Her lashes fluttered enticingly against her cheeks when she couldn't look him in the eye any longer.

"Hard isn't it?" he asked.

Her chin lifted. "I—you're not going to like what I'm going to say. You won't be able to handle it."

"Why don't you let me decide that?"

The drama room door burst open and Ty waved his arms. "We're on."

Jennifer couldn't believe the timing—she was so relieved, she went to move past John but he reached out, caging her in with a look that was almost frantic.

"It's time," her voice scraped.

"It's time you talk, Vien."

"We have to get on stage."

"Not till you talk." His other arm blocked her when she tried to dart free. He looked so reckless and audacious, so completely hot hovering over her all masculine and stretched tight. And he had that same

185 ♕

look in his eye Alex had when he'd wanted her kiss. *Power*, she thought, feeling it in a delicious current that warmed her everywhere.

She shot one fast glance over his shoulder, saw that the drama room was almost empty. Ty stood at the door ushering stragglers out with a wave of his hand. She looked up into John's face, at his lips, and lifted to her toes. Quick as a butterfly sampling a flower she kissed him.

His eyes were closed when she drew back. His lips barely parted. She pressed her back into the corner and waited for him to open his eyes.

They finally fluttered open. He looked at her so intensely her insides trembled.

Ty cleared his throat. "Guys."

"Hold on," John snapped to Ty. He didn't even look at him. It was as if he wasn't ready to let go of her or the moment—she wasn't sure which—but her knees wouldn't hold her up if he kept looking at her that way, if she was locked in this hot, steamy corner with him.

John stepped back, his arms dropping to his sides. Jennifer took in a breath, not sure if she should smile or run. He was blank, unreadable. Shocked probably, she thought, suddenly mortified at what she'd done. *I shouldn't have kissed him, it was stupid, rash.*

Before either one of them could take another breath she ducked out of the corner and left the room.

Art mirrored life. Jennifer had one moment to think as she stood on the balcony as Juliet and John hung from the trellis as Romeo. Trish, Juliet's nurse, said her lines, unaware that Romeo was hidden on the lattice, climbing to meet her in secret.

Jennifer had a flash of John falling from the rotted, vine-infested lattice he'd tried to climb outside her bedroom window. The prank had awakened her heart and made her realize just how she really felt for him.

When Trish said her last line and exited, Jennifer leaned over the balcony and saw him. A rush of excitement coursed through her.

"Then, window, let day in and let life out."

He smiled. For a flash, she dared to think the smile wasn't purely theatrical. *"Farewell, farewell. One kiss, and I'll descend."* He climbed carefully, pausing at the railing.

Jennifer cupped his cheeks, something she had never done during this scene in rehearsal, and the move sent his eyes wide. The audience quieted. The startled look on his face was priceless. Pausing, she dragged out the tension. He was helpless to stop her. The surge of momentary power brought mischief to her mind and she lowered her mouth to his.

His breath stopped. She felt him swallow, it caused his lips to move under hers and she smiled when she drew back, taking another pause at his ear to whisper, "Beat that."

Stepping back, she delivered her lines as if nothing unscripted had occurred between them. *"O God, I have an ill-divining soul. Me thinks I see thee now, thou art so low as one dead in the bottom of a tomb. Either my eyesight fails, or thou look'st pale."*

There was a fleeting flash of something playful on his face before he backed down one step, narrowing his eyes. "*And trust me, love,*" Romeo replied but it was John's taunting that sparkled in his tone, "*in my eye, so do you. Dry sorrow drinks our blood. Adieu, adieu!*"

Jennifer readied for her next line, facing the audience. She happened to catch her parents and John's parents in the front row. Seeing them broke her concentration, not expecting them there for another performance. The brilliance of white roses sat across her mother's lap.

"*O fortune, fortune!*" she began. "*All men call thee fickle. If thou art fickle, what dost thou do with him that is renowned for faith? Be fickle, fortune, for then, I hope, thou wilt not keep him long, but send him back.*" How ironic.

After finishing the lengthy scene, she darted offstage and right into John, blocking her exit. He wore a devil's grin.

"What was that?" His head jerked toward the set in reference to the kiss.

"That was me, being Juliet."

"You're so going to explain that, Vienn," he said.

"Maybe. But right now I'm needed onstage and I have to change." She tore past him. It was rousing to do something like he did with all of those spontaneous kisses during rehearsals. She took the upper hand and left his satisfyingly empty.

Something undeniably playful was in the air, infusing everyone from the players to the crew handling props. Free from the noose of consequence that had hung over previous performances, anything was possible.

Somebody lit the torches that Romeo, Paris and the Page carried with long-lasting oil, which meant when the Page was supposed to extinguish them they flickered and burned bright. The joke threw the boys off, accustomed to blowing once and having the flames go out. Andrew had the presence of mind to lay the torch down and stomp his out. John and Jake did the same. The audience laughed when all three finally had to jump on the skittering flames to extinguish them.

Money used during previous performances was somehow misplaced, forcing someone to reach into their own pocket and draw out a twentieth-century bill for an eighteenth-century exchange.

Jennifer stole the note Romeo was supposed to read and give to Paris and wrote: BEAT THIS. She watched from the sidelines when John opened it. His face didn't change as his eyes skimmed the letter, but Andrew did a double take and the hiccup nearly threw off the timing of the dialog.

In a moment of brilliance, John replaced Jennifer's vial of "poison" with colored vinegar. Jennifer's face contorted only briefly before she fell into her "death sleep."

After the scene ended she ran from the stage, seeking him out. He waited for her in the wings, his grin so big she wanted to slug him.

"Beat that," he tossed.

Her mouth pickled and puckered. "It's you who has to kiss me again. Don't blame me if I taste sour."

During the fight between Andrew and John, Jennifer held her breath. As the two boys danced up the stairs, their weapons crashing and clanging, her chest tightened with anticipation. John was so fluid, so natural. It was easy to believe he was Romeo, that he fought for something he wanted.

In a forceful strike, Andrew knocked the rapier from John's grip and sent it spinning. The weapon slid across the stage and dropped onto floor in the front row of the auditorium. Without a break, John shook a fist at Andrew then strode across the stage, leapt down and plucked up the rapier. He returned to the stage, picking up where they left off.

Perfect. Jennifer sighed with awe. *Instinctively reactive.* She glanced at his dad's face, pleased to see a smile of pride on his lips.

She took her place in the tomb and waited for John to open it. Listening to the dialogue, heaviness grew in her heart. This was the last kiss she and John would share. She wouldn't feel his body wrapped around her again. He was right today in class; *she had held back.*

Curled in a ball beneath the set she fought tears. It was almost over. The emptiness of finality came at her head on.

She heard Andrew fall and readied herself for John to open the tomb. She hoped she could keep the tears welling behind her eyes from falling.

"A grave? Oh, no. A lantern, slaughtered youth. For here lies Juliet, and her beauty makes this vault a feasting presence full of light. Death, lie thou there, by a dead man interred."

The last monologue was long, but John wasn't thinking about that as the words spilled from his mouth. After he placed Andrew near Jennifer, the finality of the show coming to a close caused emotion to swell in waves inside of him.

"Thee here in the dark to be his paramour? For fear of that, I still will stay with thee, and never from this palace of dim night depart again. Here, here I will remain."

Lifting Jennifer into his arms he slowed the monologue down, letting go of each word one last time. What he felt at that moment, thunder and storm, light and warmth was more real than theatrical.

Tears broke again and he finished with a heartfelt sob, clinging to her, kissing her longer this time. Opening the vial, he threw his head back. The crisp, bite of club soda sizzled down his throat. The shared joke left him with hope.

He fell across her in a heap and lay still as the rest of the play finished.

He didn't listen to the words spoken, he was hardly aware of the other actors moving through space around him. Under his body lay Jennifer's, warm and soft. Her breathing so faint, he had to freeze his own to assure himself she was taking in air.

Her heart beat where his chest lay across hers; the thuds seemed to seep through their clothing and join his. Stirring inside to the rhythm was something he wouldn't let go of when the curtain fell for the last time.

"A glooming peace this morning with it brings. The sun, for sorrow, will not show his head. Go hence, to have more talk of these sad things. Some shall be pardoned, and some punished. For never was there a story of more woe that this of Juliet and her Romeo."

SEVENTEEN

Tradition demanded the players and crew stay after the final performance and take down the sets. Chip ordered ten pizzas and twenty liters of soda. Somebody brought a boombox and various soundtracks pounded along with the thud of hammers, the crash of wood as it splintered and fell to the floor.

It was hard to see the set come apart; the place where days and weeks and hours had created a world that had lived for a brief moment.

Lacey took pictures, so did Fletcher and Andrew. Ann Naeverson was on hand in case somebody got hurt. She wiggled to the beat, lending a helping hand conveniently close to wherever Chip worked.

Stories were exchanged as groups worked together, respectfully tearing apart the framework of what would forever remain only in memory.

"Remember how hard it was to learn the dance?" somebody called out.

"Who choreographed that?"

"Chip."

"Not true," Chip yelled from somewhere. "Jenn helped."

Jennifer curtseyed before picking up the push broom.

"Let's have an awards party."

"Best actor, actress, stuff like that?"

"Yeah."

"Don't forget best director," Chip said, coming out from behind the main wall of the set, wiping his forehead with a bandana.

"That's definitely you," Ann Naeverson piped. Chip's cheeks reddened.

"Who sold the most tickets?" Jennifer asked.

Chip looked at Ty. "Ty?"

The stage manager pulled a piece of paper out of his back pocket. He studied it, his head tilting back and forth, lips silently counting. Then he looked up and smiled. "John."

Cheers and whistles filled the air. Everybody left their posts to congratulate him. Jennifer went to him with her broom and a grin. "Told ya."

His grin sparkled with something private, but she pushed that aside, too afraid to believe it was for her.

"Guys, she's ready to come down." The boys followed Chip to the main flat that had been both the wall of the city and the back of town. Chip directed who should stand where, who got the honor of shoving and who got to be there to make sure that when the set crashed no one was behind it.

Jennifer grabbed Lacey, Trish and Taunia, elbowing in next to the boys.

"No way." John shot her a sharp look.

"We can help." Jennifer placed her hands on the wood and held.

John's eyes flashed with fiery colors. He shook his head. "Get away."

"That's not fair," Trish whined.

"It's full-on chauvinistic," added Lacey. None of the girls were willing to leave. In fact, the rest had gathered, trying to find places where they could hone in.

Chip stepped back and clapped his hands. "Girls, girls. Thanks for the offer but I'm gonna let the guys take this one down. Come on. I have to insist." The girls didn't go willingly and made their displeasure known with a few groans.

John shot Jennifer a triumphant look over his shoulder.

The girls stood back, watching anxiously as Chip barked out orders. After a few heaves, the giant wall tumbled. Dust filled the air. Cloudy smoke floated heavenward.

The cast and crew began to break the large piece into smaller sections.

"That was cruel, putting vinegar in my vial." Jennifer stood next to John and some of the boys who were tugging the lattice off.

"Dude. Sick," somebody said.

"You didn't have to kiss me afterward, either." Jennifer reached for a section, grabbed and yanked.

"So how was it?" Drake asked John, tossing a hunk of lattice over his shoulder.

Swoons filled the air, mixing with the music of Moulin Rouge. The boys elbowed John, who turned red. He let out a grunt and pulled off another piece of lattice.

"Sour or sweet?" someone asked.

This was John's chance to strike back. He had every right to. A sinking feeling hovered over Jennifer. He kept his eyes on his hands. With more fervor, another piece came off and he threw it over his shoulder. When he didn't respond, no one pressed him for more.

As the evening wore past midnight, some said goodbye. The trailers were loaded with sets, costumes and props. More of the production family sloughed away into night as the end crept silently in.

At two a.m. Chip told those who remained they could go home. Most did, but John, Fletcher and Andrew stayed to help close the trailers up until the next morning when Chip's brother-in-law would come and drive them to wherever they were going.

Jennifer took one last walk around the clean stage. Her footsteps echoed softly in the emptiness left behind. She could still see the sets, vibrant, colorful, alive with the smell of fresh paint. Whirling in her head were dancers, their skirts flowing as music roused. Laughter rang off the corners of her mind—smiling faces. Sword fights. Pranks. And tears.

"Think you'll go out for drama in college?"

She looked across the stage at John, standing alone, his student council jacket casually tucked under his arm. She'd grown accustomed to his tights, tunic and the white blousy shirt he wore in costume whenever they were on stage. His faded jeans and light blue teeshirt looked completely twenty-first century.

"Maybe." She took a few steps his direction. "It's hard when it's all over."

"Yeah," he nodded. "Can I catch a ride home?"

"Still grounded?"

He smiled, nodded again. They began the long walk through the empty halls of the school. Neither spoke. The strange quiet of a hall characteristically full of activity left Jennifer with an odd echo of finality.

Night air chilled Jennifer and she shivered. Without warning, she felt the heavy comfort of John's jacket set loosely on her shoulders. She looked at him. "Aren't you cold?"

He shook his head, a faint smile playing on his lips. "I want you to have it."

She slipped her arms in, and pulled the coat tight. It was still warm. "I don't know why I'm cold."

"Coming down from a three month adrenalin rush will do it to you."

She dug in her purse for keys. He stood next to her by the door. Her fingers fumbled through the disorganized contents of her bag. Finally, she felt the statue of liberty key chain and pulled it out. His gaze was so intense, she stopped.

"I lied about moving," he said.

She almost dropped her keys. "You guys are moving?"

He shook his head. "In class, when I said what I was in denial about. That was only part of the truth."

"Oh." She swallowed, wanting to feel relieved, but something bigger surrounded them, bubbling and jumping with electricity.

"I was afraid to say it." His eyes looked steadily into hers, giving her courage.

"I was too," she offered. It pleased her when the tightness on his face softened. "Let me," she said, taking a deep breath, plunging shaky hands into the pockets of his coat. "I was in denial about you." She couldn't finish her admittance looking into his eyes, kind as they were. That was asking too much of herself. "I like you, John." She held her breath, held every muscle in her body in a tight, frightened fist, waiting for him to respond.

Even if he patted her head patronizingly, or laughed out loud like she was foolish, she didn't care. The weight she had carried on her back for so long was gone now. She lifted her gaze to his. Pleasure flickered in his eyes.

"I feel the same," he said.

"You do?"

He nodded.

Every sense tickled with butterflies, now free to fly through her system.

"I wanted you to say it." He touched her lightly on the arm.

"First?"

He laughed, nodding. "Yeah." He stepped closer. She felt him from her shaking knees to trembling breasts, now pressed flush against him. His fingers framed her face.

He looked at her lips. "I can't wait to kiss you."

"But you have kissed me," her voice jittered.

He shook his head as he neared. His lips floated softly over hers. "Those were for Juliet."

ABOUT
THE
AUTHOR

Jennifer Laurens has six children.
She enjoys writing, reading, traveling and miniatures.

For excerpts from her next book or to contact her,
stop by her website: www.jenniferlaurens.org

Other titles:

Magic Hands
Nailed
Heavenly

LaVergne, TN USA
29 September 2010
198864LV00001B/41/P